MONSTER NANNY

Dedicated to
Leonardo and Maikki

www.hmhco.com

The text was set in Adobe Garamond Pro.

Library of Congress Cataloging-in-Publication Data
Names: Tolonen, Tuutikki, 1975–author. | Pitkänen, Pasi, illustrator. |
Silver, Annira, translator.
Title: Monster nanny / by Tuutikki Tolonen ; illustrated by Pasi Pitkänen ;
translation by Annira Silver.
Other titles: Mèorkèovahti. English
Description: Boston ; New York : Houghton Mifflin Harcourt, [2017] |
Summary: When their mother wins a trip while their father is away,
Halley, Koby, and Mimi's lives are turned upside-down by a
hairy, smelly, half-troll nanny.
Identifiers: LCCN 2016037228 | ISBN 9780544943544 (hardcover)
Subjects: | CYAC: Nannies—Fiction. | Monsters—Fiction. | Brothers and
sisters—Fiction. | Adventure and adventurers—Fiction.
Classification: LCC PZ7.1.T624 Mon 2017 | DDC [Fic]—dc23
LC record available at https://lccn.loc.gov/2016037228

Manufactured in the United States of America
DOC 10 9 8 7 6 5 4 3 2 1
4500677655

English edition published by agreement with Tuutikki Tolonen,
Pasi Pitkänen, and Elina Ahlback Agency, Helsinki, Finland.

MONSTER NANNY

by Tuutikki Tolonen

Illustrated by Pasi Pitkänen

Translated by Annira Silver

HOUGHTON MIFFLIN HARCOURT

BOSTON NEW YORK

CONTENTS

CHAPTER 1

The Fateful Breakfast

A S SO OFTEN HAPPENS, it all started in the morning. Mom was wiping down the sink with a small sponge. The Hellman children — Halley, eleven, Koby, nine, and Mimi, six years and four months — were sitting at the round kitchen table, eating corn flakes.

The news was on the radio: *Schools have let out for the summer, warm weather on the way, weekend traffic running smoothly . . .*

Mom's sponge hovered above the sink as she turned to the children. She was nervous and for a good reason.

"It's the morning of my departure, but the train tickets still haven't come," she complained. "I'm sure that grand prize drawing win was a hoax. Trip to Lapland and two weeks of relaxing treatments! Too good to be true. Such things just don't happen."

Mom turned back to the sink and continued scrubbing while mumbling, "But I still believed it. I even packed my suitcase all ready, but there's no sign of the tickets."

The children looked at one another.

"And by the way, no sign of the nanny, either," Halley said.

"No sign of the nanny," Mom repeated.

"Nor Invisible Voice," Mimi continued.

Mom frowned.

"But Invisible Voice is often *heard*," Koby corrected Mimi.

"One who is heard a lot doesn't need to be seen," Halley giggled.

"Stop that Invisible Voice nonsense," Mom said

sternly. "Dad's coming home tonight, as you well know. He's already on the plane."

"I don't think he's on the plane," Halley whispered to Koby. Invisible Voice was not very good at coming home on time.

"What are you whispering?" Mom asked.

"Nothing," Koby answered quickly.

The doorbell rang.

"Here they are!" Mom exclaimed. She looked around. The kitchen was still messy.

"I'll get it," Halley said, jumping up. Mom quickly swiped the breakfast crumbs off the table with the sponge and hurried to the hall after Halley.

The postman stood at the door. He was not the usual postman, but smarter-looking and more energetic. He wore a yellow jacket, gray baseball cap, and gray tie. He had definitely not ridden to their street on the post office bike.

"I wonder if Mary Hellman is at home?" he asked politely. "I have a package. Someone must confirm receipt."

"Confirm?" Halley repeated.

"Sign," the postman explained.

Mom wiped her hands on her apron and stepped forward.

"I am Mary Hellman," she said. "I've won a trip in a prize drawing. This must be the train tickets."

The postman nodded and handed Mom a paper and pen. "Right there. And your name in capitals, if you please."

Mom signed. The postman handed her an envelope.

"Here we are. Have an excellent day!"

He raised his cap and disappeared down into the stairway.

Mom carefully tore the envelope open.

"Oh, yes, here they are," she said, relieved, and pulled a folded sheet of paper out of the envelope, with the train tickets inside.

"What does it say?" Halley asked.

Mom unfolded the sheet of paper and read out loud:

"Dear Recipient,

Once again: congratulations to the winner! At last, it is time for your trip. Time to recharge your batteries, relax, and learn new things. Time to think of your own well-being, wake up to birdsong and the tickle of the sun's rays. Welcome!

After two weeks you will be like a new person. Our relaxation camp, the exact location of which will be revealed as soon as you arrive, starts tomorrow at noon. The camp duration is exactly two weeks, and in all that time you will need no money, just warm clothing and an energetic camping mindset. After the two weeks, you will be returned to your home, unless you choose to go to some

*other place. The special camp train leaves the central
railway station at eight p.m. today. Please, do not be late.
Your train tickets are enclosed."*

"Special camp train!" Halley echoed. "Looks like
Mom wasn't the only one to win a relaxation trip."

"Idiot, the others must pay for it themselves, of course,"
Koby corrected her. "Isn't that right, Mom?"

Mom didn't reply but stared at the letter. Her brow
became strangely crinkled.

"What else does it say?" Halley asked.

"Hell's bells," Mom grumbled. "It says here that
because your dad travels for work, the nanny will stay
day and night until I get back. Two weeks, night and
day!"

"Didn't you tell them that Invisible Voice is coming
home?" Koby asked. "I mean, that Dad's coming?"

"I thought it was self-evident!" Mom said.

"Are we having a nanny move in?" Mimi asked,
delighted. She liked all the staff at the daycare center.

"They never said anything about nights," Mom muttered. "I thought we'd get someone who tidies up and
cooks dinner a few times a week. This is a different thing
altogether."

"Is Invisible Voice's coming home canceled?" Halley
whispered to Koby.

Koby shrugged. He really didn't know.

"They should have made this clear before," Mom went on, shaking her head. "A total stranger! Where do we put her in this place? We haven't got a guest room."

"Your bed will be free," Mimi piped up.

"This has gotten too complicated," Mom said, not happy. Then she was quiet again and continued reading.

"What else does it say?" Koby asked, when Mom's lips suddenly clamped together in a tight line.

"Read it out loud!" Mimi said, agitated.

"And what is this supposed to mean?" Mom asked in a startled voice, and read:

"You will have the opportunity to participate in a secret special experiment, in which we are researching new options for child care work. The nanny that will arrive at your home is a half-human fully trained for the job—"

"Half-human!" yelled Mimi. "What? Read it again!"

"Mimi, don't yell," Halley asked. "Mom, please read on."

Mom continued:

". . . half-human, according to an old definition, a monster or a troll . . ."

Halley suppressed a giggle.

"This is a prank!"

"Candid Camera." Koby grinned, peering around the room.

But Mimi watched Mom, thrilled. Tickling, happy thrilled. Could it be true? A monster in her home. Nanny and monster.

Mom's voice was tense as she went on:

"We would like to stress that the creature is safe. However, the experiment is very confidential, and under no circumstances must you tell anyone about the creature. A breach of this obligation for confidentiality results in a set penalty. Moreover, we wish to remind you that when you accepted this prize, you signed a confidentiality agreement . . ."

Mom raised her eyes from the letter. She looked cross.

"That agreement didn't say anything about half-humans and monsters!" she griped. "I thought that I mustn't tell anybody about the kinds of relaxation treatments they do! This is a completely different matter. My children are not guinea pigs. Nobody sets any penalties on me in my own home."

"I can keep a secret!" Mimi shouted. "I want the half-human to come here!"

"Mimi, don't shout," Koby said.

Just then the doorbell rang again.

"For goodness' sake," Mom said angrily.

Halley stepped to the door and opened it. A total shocked silence descended on the hall.

At the door stood a brown-black creature. It was big and wide and almost filled the whole doorway. But what was it? It had two enormous feet, on which it stood solidly in place. It had two enormous hands. Its palms were like saucepan lids, and each of its four fingers like a fat barbecue sausage. In one of its hands, the creature held a crumpled scrap of paper.

But did it have a thick, matted fur coat, or was it wearing a coverall made from ragged scraps of cloth? A strange smell, reminiscent of a musty cellar, spread into the hall. The creature rolled its big, round yellow eyes and grunted something. Mimi hid behind Mom.

Behind the creature stood a messenger in a gray suit, a different man from the earlier one. He nodded a nervous greeting, cleared his throat, and said: "This has been sent to you. Can you sign, please?"

He slid an electronic receipt device past the creature and handed it to Mom. Mom stared at the creature, her mouth slightly open.

"Mom, sign your name," Halley said, and nudged her gently.

"What do we do with that?" Mom asked.

"It comes with instructions," the messenger answered, and coughed.

"Go on, sign," Halley repeated.

"What if I don't want it?" Mom asked quietly.

"There are no actual alternatives," the messenger said. "I was told to bring this here. There is no return address."

"Go on, Mom, just sign," Halley said.

"Well, if it definitely comes with instructions," Mom murmured, sighing.

She signed the screen in slightly shaky handwriting. The messenger snatched his device back. "Have a very nice day," he said quickly, and slipped away.

The Hellman family and their new nanny stood at the door like statues. Halley stared at the creature. Koby stared at the creature. Mom's eyes flitted now to the creature, now to her children, because she didn't know whether or not the children should be quickly saved and if so, how, since they were on the fifth floor of a large apartment building and the creature filled the whole doorway, so there was no way out.

"Mom, is that the monster?" Mimi whispered from behind Mom's back.

The creature let out a hollow grunt and pushed the scrap of paper at Halley, who happened to be standing nearest to it. Halley hesitantly took the paper.

The creature grunted again. Mom caught her breath,

startled. Halley unfolded the paper. It was tatty, grubby, and a bit torn. A little lump of soil fell out of it and crumbled on the floor.

"This must be the instructions," Halley said. Mom frowned.

"What does it say?" Koby asked.

Halley read out loud:

*"**Receiving family:** Hellman.*

***Sent:** Trained half-human, commonly known as a 'monster.'*

***Specialty:** Child care and domestic work.*

***Character:** Not violent, likes TV, is happy in human houses.*

***Other notes:** No proper name, addressed as 'monster nanny' or simply 'monster.' Finds its own food outdoors during darkness. NB: Never leaves children home alone!*

***English-language skills:** Poor. Understands a little, does not speak. Language skills not expected to improve. NB: Lack of language does not affect ability to work.*

***Accommodation:** Hall closet (closet to be emptied immediately)."*

"Oh, for Pete's sake," Mom snapped. "I wonder how this'll end?"

Halley and Koby looked at each other. Interesting indeed. How would it end?

Mimi sidled out from behind Mom's skirt. She looked at the monster and smiled.

"It's not dangerous," Mimi said, putting out her little hand to the monster. "Look at its eyes. It wants to stay here."

CHAPTER 2

Talking with Invisible Voice

T HEY HAD TO REMOVE the shelves from the hall closet before the monster would fit.

"And where do we put all this junk?" Mom asked. The contents of the closet lay in two heaps on the hall floor. Nobody answered. Mom frowned and looked at the monster.

"All right, let's try it. Get in, get in."

The monster squeezed into the closet. The closet was quite narrow. To fit in it, the monster had to stand straight with its arms tightly at its sides, but it didn't seem bothered by the lack of room. The monster growled contentedly.

"It looks like a cigar," Halley said.

"A hairy cigar," Koby continued.

"Dirt cigar!" Mimi giggled.

"Children," Mom scolded them, but she couldn't take her eyes off the monster either. Small clumps of earth seemed to be dropping off it all the time. The whole hallway was covered in gray earth dust. Soon the whole apartment would resemble a potato cellar, of which it already smelled.

The phone rang.

"Invisible Voice," Halley said, pleased. "I'll get it."

"I'm sure it can't be Dad. He's flying over the Atlantic right now," Mom said, subdued, and picked up the receiver.

"Hellman residence," she answered.

Her face immediately took on a horrified expression.

"Sam! What on earth? Why aren't you on the plane?"

Halley nodded knowingly at Koby.

"What did I tell you?" she whispered.

"No, I did," Koby whispered back.

Mom was listening, worried. "I see. I see. Really bad timing, Sam. You see, we had a delivery of . . . Oh, you already know?"

"That's what it said in the letter," Koby commented, nodding to Halley.

"Well, it looks . . ." Mom began, and glanced at the monster, which was contentedly rubbing its back against the back of the closet. Dust was flying around it.

"It's . . . pretty earthy. Perhaps it ought to be washed. It looks quite happy there in the closet. Yes, the closet, here in the hall. That's where it had to be put."

Mom was silent for a long while, listening. She crinkled her brow, disconcerted.

"But did you hear that on top of everything else, this is some kind of an experiment?" Mom demanded. "They want to use our children to test whether or not this kind of creature can be a good caretaker. What if it turns out that it isn't? What happens then? I'm canceling the trip to Lapland. I can't go."

Mom cast her eyes at the monster, who had suddenly dropped off to sleep on its feet. At least its eyes were closed, and it was leaning against the back of the closet, breathing peacefully.

"Mom, we'll be OK," Halley interjected. "You can go off to Lapland, no problem."

"Dad wants to speak to you," Mom said, handing the phone to Halley.

"Hey," Halley began. "Well, it smells of a potato cellar. It's not very big, kind of . . . fits in the closet. It doesn't matter! We're not a bit scared. When are you coming? A blizzard? That's weird. A blizzard in June. Never heard of such a thing."

Koby rolled his eyes. Halley didn't realize that it isn't summer everywhere in June. In some places, it's even winter. Depends on what part of the world you happen to be in.

"Less soccer and more reading, Halley," Koby said. Halley stuck out her tongue at him and continued talking to her father.

"The fridge is full of food! OK. Wait a sec." Halley

handed the phone to Koby. "Invisible Voice wants to talk to you."

Koby took the phone. "Hello. What? Uh, Halley didn't say anything." Koby made a face at Halley. Invisible Voice didn't like being called Invisible Voice. "Of course I know how to make a meal. At least make sandwiches and peel mandarin oranges. Of course we'll manage. Halley knows how to do everything. Probably even . . . well, even make oatmeal! Mimi? I don't know. Ask Mimi. If you're coming on the very next flight, it's only the one night. Yeah, yeah. A good plan. OK, bye then."

Koby passed the phone to Mimi. "Mimi," he said. "*He* wants to talk to you."

Mimi took the phone.

"Hello, who is this? Invisible Voice? So, you're not coming, then? What?" Mimi chattered, and grinned at Mom, who was frowning.

"Well, it doesn't matter! We did guess. Well, of course! I'm not scared to be at home. Halley and Koby and the bathrobe are here. Yes, it still talks. It's the best bathrobe ever."

Mom shook her head. She didn't think Dad needed to know everything that happened in the house. Some of the strangest things could easily be swept up in a dustpan and chucked off the balcony into the yard before anyone even noticed they had existed. Like Mimi's talking bathrobe. Mom's breathing started to tighten at the mere thought of it. She really did need this Lapland holiday.

Mimi chattered on, giggling happily.

"Well, it's a monster! It does look quite real. It's got yellow eyes. No . . . I'll go and see." Mimi peeked in the monster's closet. "The nails are quite short. Really dirty, though. You'll see when you get here." Mimi listened for a moment. "Yes, yes. No, *that's* the bathrobe. It's not a toy. Good, we'll do that!"

Mimi handed the receiver back to Mom.

"Hello," Mom said into the phone. "Of course it works. You're calling it now. Yes, they are big kids." Mom measured the children with her eyes. "We'll do that. Call again soon. No, you. You always do the calling. OK, bye then. Three minutes."

Mom hung up the call. "Children," she said. "You already heard that your dad's plane was unable to take off. He said — "

"That bathrobes don't talk," Mimi interrupted with a grin.

"No, but that the next flight leaves in a few hours and arrives here tomorrow during the day. Dad will be on it, but will you manage until then with *that?*"

Mom nodded at the closet.

"Of course," Halley answered. "But what do we do when Invisible Voice comes?"

"Whatever do you mean?" Mom asked.

"That maybe we could check out a photo so we know what Invisible Voice looks like? So we know we're opening the door to the right person?" Koby went on, and Halley tittered.

Mom rolled her eyes.

"Stop it. He is your father. He has a traveling job! Do you think he wants to be away all the time? You know he doesn't. Stop those silly jokes. Dad wanted me to ask you if you're all right to stay here with that creature until he gets back tomorrow. Or shall we think of something else?"

"Of course we're all right," Halley replied. "It's a reliable nanny. That's what it says on that piece of paper."

"We really *want* to stay alone with it," Mimi assured her.

"Koby, what do you think?" Mom said. Koby looked at the steadily breathing, sleeping monster. It didn't look dangerous. Still, it felt weird that the monster would be looking after them. But whatever. Exciting things were supposed to happen during summer vacation.

"I'm sure we'll be fine," Koby said.

The phone rang again. Three minutes had passed. Invisible Voice was particular about telephone timings. Mom picked up.

"Hello. Hey. Yes, we did. The children say they'll manage. It is strange, to be sure. Yes. But it can't be helped. You have your key?"

The children looked at one another. Halley let out a quiet whistle. Strange things were happening. Mom, who never went anywhere, was going away. Dad, who was never at home, was coming back. The children, who had never been left alone, were about to spend the night on their own. And in the hall closet slept a trained monster, though everybody had always been told that monsters didn't exist.

"I'm going to take a bath now," said Mimi.

Halley and Koby nodded. It was good that at least one thing was just as before.

CHAPTER 3

Mom Really Does Leave

THE VACUUM CLEANER IS there. As you know. And the kitchen sponge is in the bottom cupboard. And all the cleaning stuff . . ."

Koby was looking at the white walls and white ceiling in their home. Very odd. It was as if there was a new gray shade everywhere. It came from the monster, of course. Even though the monster had only been in the house for a few hours and was in the closet almost the whole time, it had managed to shed enough of some weird substance to coat the entire apartment. It wasn't dirt, despite Mom thinking it was. It wasn't any known substance. It was a bit like mist in the air. Or darkness stuck to the walls.

"Monster dust," Koby said to himself, and rubbed the wall with his finger. Minute gray specks were stuck to his finger.

"Koby, are you listening to me?" Mom asked. "Yes, the mop is there between the closet and the wall—can you see . . ." she went on.

Koby nodded in agreement. He knew where everything was. He had lived in this apartment all his life. She didn't need to explain where the mop was kept. Right now Koby should have been at the library looking for information on monsters, not getting a refresher course on housecleaning. Mom had only let Halley go to the library because Halley was the eldest. Naturally, it was a mistake, because age is not the same thing as research skills.

Koby sighed. Totally idiotic. What was the point of sending Halley to the library? She was useless. She could never find anything, whereas Koby knew precisely what was to be found on every shelf. He knew what to ask for. Now he would have to go back to the library later, to get all the right books, which, no doubt, Halley would leave on the shelves.

Mom looked at the clock on the wall. The sound of Mimi talking to her bathrobe came from the bathroom.

"I wonder how all this will end. What is keeping Halley? I've got to go soon. Good thing the bags are packed and the food shopping done. I'll go and wash Mimi's hair now," Mom said, talking to herself.

"No!" Mimi shrieked from the bathroom. How did she always hear everything? Mom sighed.

"Same fight every time. But your hair has to be washed. Or you'll get nits."

"Head lice are not linked to hair washing at all. They crawl slowly from one head to the next," Koby said.

Mom sighed again.

"Could you not say that just for once? It's hard enough to get Mimi's hair washed."

"One should not present false arguments," Koby said.

"Well, you present correct arguments, then. Convince Mimi," Mom said, walking off into the kitchen. "I'll set the table in the meantime. Tell her I'll be there in three minutes. And I don't intend to fight over her hair being washed."

Koby peeked into the bathroom. Mimi was sitting in her bubble bath. She was totally immersed in a conversation, the other party of which sat on the toilet seat, right next to the bathtub: Mimi's blue bathrobe. It sat upright and alert, hood perky, just as if there were something other than air inside it.

It used to be Koby's bathrobe, but back then it had been quite ordinary. Now it had changed. Sometimes Koby wondered why this had happened. Was it his fault? Why had the robe never spoken to him? It talked to Mimi all the time. Koby would definitely have been more interesting to talk to. Mimi was basically a little bit daft. Or at least a bit strange.

"I think it's kind, you know?" Mimi was saying. "It does stink badly. Like a rotten potato. And Mom doesn't like that dust at all. It's probably asleep in the closet even now. Probably sleeps quite a lot. You what?"

The bathrobe waved its empty sleeve. It was gesturing, like lively talkers do. There was no sound. Only Mimi could hear the bathrobe's voice. Koby could see it move. Sometimes. Nobody else ever saw anything other than a limp waffle-cloth bathrobe that lay in an untidy heap in any odd place.

"Really?" Mimi replied to the bathrobe. Clearly, she had heard something surprising. The bathrobe continued its voiceless speech and Mimi wrinkled her brow, deep in thought. *I wonder what the bathrobe said,* Koby pondered. Mimi nodded and laughed.

"Yeah, right! Of course it's nice to see Invisible Voice. Kind of. And a bit strange. I can't quite remember what he looks like. What if he's horribly ugly or scary? Like with a scarred face and wearing a pirate hat?"

The bathrobe shifted its position. It seemed to concentrate on listening.

"I'm sure I'm going to miss Mom," Mimi said, frowning. "Lucky there's Koby and Halley. So I don't have to be alone. Shame they're so dumb."

"You're the one who's dumb, talking to a bathrobe," Koby snapped through the slightly open door.

Quick as lightning, Mimi turned toward the door. The bathrobe slipped into a limp heap of cloth on the toilet seat and didn't say anything more.

"You numskull!" Mimi shouted. "Look what you've done—you frightened it! And we were having a conversation."

Koby shrugged. "Let Mom wash your hair, and then you can talk to it in peace and quiet again," he said. Mimi made a face.

"Are we ready in here?" Mom asked behind Koby at the door.

"All ready," Koby said. Mimi gave him a vicious look but didn't struggle anymore.

"See," Koby said to Mom. "Correct arguments."

"You are one peculiar boy," Mom said.

"No, I'm not," Koby said. "Mimi is peculiar. I'm just sensible."

Mom nodded slowly. She looked at Mimi sitting in the midst of her bubbles and Koby leaning on the door frame. Her amazing children. Her peculiar, wise, fine children.

How had they become like that? Mom closed her eyes and took a deep breath. Now she'd wash Mimi's hair and try to forget the stinking monster in the hall closet.

The key rattled in the lock. Halley! Koby quickly slipped away from the bathroom door and ran into the hall. Sounds of running water, Mimi's angry protests, and Mom's tired sighs emanated from the bathroom.

Halley's cheeks glowed with excitement as she dropped a heavy bag of books on the hall rug. She flung her green baseball cap in the general direction of the coat hooks, grinning at Koby mysteriously.

"Having a bath?" she whispered.

"Hair washing," Koby replied quickly.

"Good," Halley whispered, and called loudly in the direction of the bathroom: "Hey! I'm back!"

"Hey!" Mom called, surrounded by running water noise.

"What did you find?" Koby asked quietly. Halley looked pleased.

"Only children's picture books at first, but then, luckily, I had the good sense to look on another shelf."

"Let me see," Koby said hurriedly.

Halley glanced at the bathroom door. The running water had stopped.

"Let me dry you," Mom said, coaxing Mimi.

"No!" Mimi yelled.

"Best not to let Mom see it. Believe me," Halley

whispered. "She might not go if she sees this book. It's pretty . . . fantastic."

Koby nodded in agreement. "All right."

Halley dragged the bookbag into their bedroom and hid it behind a box of toy cars. Mimi pattered into the room, dripping wet and cross, in her blue bathrobe.

"You lied to me!" she hissed to Koby. "Mom wouldn't let me stay in the bath anymore. I can't talk to the bathrobe if I'm *wearing* it!"

Koby shrugged.

"Now everybody in for supper! I've got to go in half an hour," Mom called from the bathroom.

"Supper? It's not even half past six," Halley said to Koby and Mimi. Koby checked his watch. True. It was 6:21.

Mom appeared at the bedroom door.

"Come along. We can't be sure when that *thing* in the closet thinks to feed you. And in any case, I'm going very soon and I'll be away for two weeks. It would be nice to have supper together before I leave."

She looked a little bit sad.

They had a very strange supper. Mom had picked out all kinds of things that the children liked: waffles with whipped cream and strawberry jam, meatballs, grapes, chocolate milk, a whistle lollipop each, chicken nuggets.

"Wow," said Koby.

"I wonder how this'll work," Mom said, shaking her head. "Two weeks is an awfully long time. Whatever was I thinking? I shouldn't have agreed to this at all."

"Two weeks is not a particularly long time," Koby remarked, helping himself to the grapes. "Just think how many weeks there are in a whole year."

"And in any case, you wanted to go to Lapland last year too. And couldn't go," Halley said, her mouth full of meatball.

"We can phone each other every day," Koby reassured her.

"We shouldn't call every day. I read in a health magazine that it's better to send text messages. Talking on the phone makes one miss people more," Mom said wretchedly.

"We'll text each other every day," Koby consoled her.

Mimi's bottom lip began to tremble. Halley quickly loaded her sister's plate full of whipped cream and strawberry jam, which melancholy Mimi started spooning up.

"Everything will be fine," Halley said to Mimi. Or perhaps she said it to all of them together. "Of course we'll manage."

There was a bang in the hall. They all jumped and turned to look in the direction of the noise. "What—" Mom started.

The hall closet door opened wide. The monster maneuvered itself out with a puff of dust. It stepped heavily to the kitchen door, stopped there, and rolled its globular yellow eyes from Mom to the children and back again.

"Grrmmmm," it grunted.

"It's woken up," Halley said.

"Goodness me!" Mom exclaimed.

"It wasn't asleep," Mimi said.

"Yes, it was," Halley answered.

"No, it was not," Mimi repeated.

"What do you mean?" Halley said.

"Does it want something to eat?" Koby asked uneasily.

"It was waiting for its shift to start. The bathrobe said that—" Mimi went on.

"Please, not the bathrobe again," Halley snapped, and Mimi fell silent.

"The taxi will be here in ten minutes," Mom said, agitated. Now that the monster was in sight again, it was much more difficult to forget it.

The monster grunted and moved away from the kitchen door.

"I'll turn on the TV for it. It said in the letter that it likes watching TV," Halley said. She jumped up and slipped past the monster into the living room.

"Wait! We need to cover the couch. I'll do it," Mom said, running after Halley. The monster remained standing at the kitchen door, looking back and forth from the living room to the kitchen.

"What did the bathrobe say?" Koby asked, turning to Mimi.

"That it once knew a monster and it was really particular about times. That it always turned up only when it was monster time. Never any other time," Mimi whispered. "And that it never slept. Never. It just waited for monster time. And it never forgot anything. *Anything*, get it?"

"No, I don't get it," Koby answered quietly.

"Neither do I," Mimi said, frowning. "Is that good or bad?"

"I don't know. We'll soon see," Koby said.

Mom carried her suitcase to the door and put her coat on. The monster sat in the living room on the sofa, which had been covered with trash bags, watching a gardening show.

"The time to go came too quickly after all," Mom muttered, worried.

Mimi hugged her leg. Halley and Koby hugged her waist. Mom tried to hug them all at the same time.

"I'm sure it'll be really lovely there," Halley mumbled, her face buried against Mom.

"I'll be OK. You'll be OK," Mom whispered. "I will miss you so terribly. Let's phone every day, OK? No, we'll send text messages. And Dad's coming tomorrow, real soon. Remember that."

Then she kissed each of her children on top of their head, let go of her hug, and picked up her suitcase.

"Bye," Mimi whispered.

"Bye," Mom whispered back. "Try to keep everything going until Dad comes."

Then Mom left. The children heard the elevator rattling toward the lower floors.

"Well," Halley said somberly. She no longer sounded quite as confident as a moment ago. "This is it, then."

"What?" Koby asked.

"This here. Us. Here we are now with that monster."

Koby and Mimi nodded. They turned their eyes toward the living room, where the monster sat motionless, like a bronze statue. The light of the evening sun flooded in through the living room window, revealing the dust flakes floating slowly through the air.

CHAPTER 4

Things You (Perhaps) Always Wanted to Know About Monsters

I T REALLY DOES LIKE watching TV," Halley whispered. The monster sat on the trash bags stretched across the couch, staring at the TV screen as if it were bewitched.

"Show me the book now," Koby said.

"What book?" Mimi asked.

"You did borrow a picture book for Mimi? One with thick cardboard pages?" Koby asked.

"Numskulls!" Mimi shouted, and made a face.

"Hush! Not so much noise," Halley said. "Come on."

They crept into the bedroom, and Halley closed the door behind them. The bookbag was waiting for them where Halley had left it. She grabbed the bag and tipped the books out as quietly as possible in the middle of the floor.

"*Monster Rhymes?*" Koby read on the cover of the first book, glancing at Halley incredulously. "*The Adventures of Honey Monster on Honey Island?*"

"Decoy books," Halley said dryly. "Take a look at this."

Halley dug a thick, old book with a brown cover from the bottom of the pile. There was no picture on the front. It smelled like a musty library cellar.

"What's that?" Mimi asked.

Halley looked at her siblings, excited. Then she read from the cover:

"*Monsters: Characteristics and Qualities of the Species in Light of My Experiences.*"

"Wow," said Koby.

"This is a scientific book. Very old, but quite authentic. Real information about real monsters," Halley explained.

"Wow," Koby said again. "Who wrote it?"

"Runar Kalli," Halley read, and turned back to Koby. "Eighty years ago. You see, he found a monster in the forest behind his house, coaxed it into his home, and studied it for almost two years. Then one day the monster vanished and was never seen again."

"So where is that monster now?" Mimi asked apprehensively. "Could it come here?"

"Oh, please, Mimi. We've got a monster there in the living room," Halley reminded her, smiling. "It's no good being scared of it now. We've just got to work out how to deal with it."

"We need information," Koby said pensively. "Tell us more, Halley."

Halley nodded solemnly and continued in a low voice: "So Runar's monster escaped, but Runar had made meticulous notes of all his research. And that research is in this book. This may be the only scientific book on monsters in the whole world."

Koby frowned. "So why does everybody think that monsters don't exist, if there's a real scientific book that you can borrow from the library?"

Halley shrugged. "I don't know. Maybe because all children are told that there are no such things as monsters. Because *nobody wants to believe in monsters*. Do you see?"

Koby nodded doubtfully.

"I wonder what happened to Runar?" he said.

"Naturally, he was labeled stark-raving mad as soon as this book came out. He was first sent to a psychiatric hospital, but then he simply disappeared."

"Disappeared?" Mimi echoed.

"Yes. Perhaps he ran away to look for his monster."

"How do you know all this?" Koby asked.

"The librarian told me," Halley said, smiling modestly.

"The librarian! How did *you* get her to talk to you?" Koby grumbled.

"So you thought she only talks to you, did you?" Halley challenged him.

"But . . ." Koby began. Because, actually, that was exactly what he had thought. That the librarian told exciting things just to him. That Koby was the librarian's special favorite, best customer, and most prolific book borrower. The boy who had read almost everything! This felt strange.

Halley stared at Koby, annoyed. Her little brother was such a know-it-all!

"All right! I said I was looking for books for you. That I'm your sister and you sent me to the library. That's why she talked to me," Halley admitted. "Happy now?"

Koby nodded slowly and felt a little more secure. More confident. It's not good if absolutely everything changes in one day. It can make one feel quite wobbly.

"What does it say in that book?" Mimi urged

impatiently. It was frustrating being the only person in the house who couldn't read.

Halley opened the book and leafed through the yellowed first pages.

"Monsters: Characteristics and Qualities of the Species in Light of My Experiences. By Runar Kalli."

"I wonder if Runar Kalli is still alive," Koby said.

"Maybe, if he's around a hundred and twenty years old," Halley said, and continued turning the pages carefully.

"Table of contents," Koby said. "Wait. What does it say?"

Halley gave Koby a bored look. Halley never read tables of contents. She had always thought that they weren't even meant to be read. Koby inched closer and read aloud over Halley's shoulder:

"Foreword to the Reader
Introduction to the Subject
PART ONE: Monsters in Stories
    Chapter 1: Earliest Descriptions of Monsters
        in Literature
    Chapter 2: Monsters in Children's Stories
    Chapter 3: Are Stories Hints of Reality?
PART TWO: Real Monsters"

"Now we're getting somewhere!" Halley said, cheering up.

"Shhh," Mimi hissed.

Koby read on:

"PART TWO: Real Monsters

"Where do we start? 'Some Unusual Observations' sounds good. And the bit about food," Halley interrupted.

"There's more still," Koby said.

"Yes, Halley. Just shut up for a bit," Mimi commanded, and settled right next to Koby to stare at the contents page.

"What idiot reads the table of contents when we have the whole book?" Halley wailed. "You are so weird!"

"No, we're clever. And you're a numskull," Mimi muttered. "Can you be quiet, please?"

Halley kept quiet, and Koby went on:

"**PART THREE: Is a Monster More Human or Animal?**
   Chapter 13: The Monster's Human-like Habits
   Chapter 14: The Monster's Animal-like Habits
   Chapter 15: Can a Monster Learn to Behave
      Like Humans?
   Chapter 16: Possible Dangers
   Chapter 17: Possible Uses and Benefits
   Chapter 18: What Is a Monster, Really?"

"That sounds really interesting too. Indeed, what *is* a monster, really? And what are the dangers?" Halley pondered aloud. "Shall we read one of those first? A really interesting book. A pretty good find, wasn't it?"

"Shhh," Mimi hissed again.

"There's still more," Koby said, and read on:

"**PART FOUR: Empirical Studies**
   Chapter 19: Measurements
   Chapter 20: Language Samples
   Chapter 21: Drawings
   Chapter 22: Extracts from Research Diary
   Postscript"

"That's the end," Mimi said, eyes on Halley.

"What does 'empirical' mean?" Halley asked.

"Studies that Runar Kalli has done. Measurements and such," Koby answered.

"We could measure our monster too," Mimi enthused.

"Where shall we start reading?" Halley asked impatiently.

"At the beginning, of course," said Koby.

"The beginning!" Halley yelled. "So why did we read the table of contents? What was the point, if we're starting at the beginning anyway? The table of contents is there so that the reader can choose what she wants to read!"

"No, the table of contents is a bit like a map. It's always good to know what's coming," Koby explained patiently.

"Hey. I think the monster is coming," Mimi whispered. "Listen."

Halley and Koby fell silent. They heard heavy footsteps approaching the door. Koby slammed the book shut and flung it under the bed. Mimi snatched up a decoy book, Halley another, Koby a third.

"Open the books," Koby whispered, flopping down on the rug in a reading position.

Exactly four seconds later, when the monster opened the door and stood in the doorway viewing its charges, all it saw were three good dear children leafing through harmless picture books.

CHAPTER 5

A Hungry Monster
in the Closet

MANY OF US KNOW what it's like to go to sleep suspecting that there is a monster under the bed. It is not nice. It is unpleasant and very nerve-racking. Falling asleep is impossible because you must keep your eyes open and your ears pricked up to the extreme.

What is it like to go to sleep knowing that there quite definitely is a monster in the hall closet? If you know that there are no adults at home but just three children? Admittedly clever and resourceful ones, but still only three children without their parents? And that there really is a monster in the hall closet?

It is awful. It is awful, even if you know (having read a certain scientific book) that monsters are not very dangerous and that on no account do they eat humans.

"Let's leave the night-light on," Koby said. All three were sitting on Halley's bed, very close to one another. Also sitting and lying on the bed were about eighty different stuffed animals—in other words, all their stuffed animals. Mimi wanted the bed really full. She felt safer that way.

"Can I sleep here, Halley?" Mimi asked softly.

"Of course," Halley said, and turned to Koby. "Do you want to come too? We can all fit. We'll move some of the toys."

"No, I'm sleeping in my own bed," Koby said bravely, even though he was not feeling particularly brave. He had read that in difficult situations you should not give in to fear, because it can easily turn into despair and spread to everybody. It was better to tell everyone (yourself included) that you were not a bit scared. That the situation was not so bad. Just a little bad. Everything would be all right, no problem.

Mimi was squashed right up against Halley. It was so quiet. No sound of the monster's footsteps, nothing at all. They wondered if Mom had arrived in Lapland yet. They had tried to call, but she hadn't answered. Then they had sent a text message that said:

> Hi, Mom. We are OK.
> The monster came out
> of the closet and made

us oatmeal for a bedtime
snack. It was good, but
Mimi didn't want to eat.
The monster does not
talk. It rolls its eyes.
We tidied up a bit. The
monster knows how
to use the dishwasher.
Everything is fine, how
are you? The monster
got back into the closet,
and we are going to bed.
H, K, and M

The bit about tidying up wasn't true, but Halley had thought that it would make Mom happy, and anyway, maybe they'd tidy up tomorrow. Besides, it wasn't worth cleaning the house every day with a monster shedding dust all over the place.

"Koby, read that bit again, where it says what monsters eat," Mimi asked quietly.

"Not again!" Halley groaned. "We've read it at least five hundred times. It won't eat you, honestly. It doesn't eat meat."

"I can read it again," Koby said good-naturedly, and pulled out the book from under the pillow.

It had taken a while to get Koby to agree to read the

book here and there instead of from the beginning. It was really only when Halley had pointed out the urgency of their situation that Koby had given in. It really was the truth. They were in an emergency situation. They didn't have time to read the whole thick book from start to finish. They had to use it like a reference book and look for information about this and that. Like about eating. It was important to know whether the monster ate people at nighttime or not. Because it was now almost midnight.

Koby expertly opened the book to page 276, "Chapter 10: Nutrition and Foraging for Food," and started reading.

"The natural diet of monsters was a mystery to me for a long time. The monster was happy to eat everything I offered it: potatoes, leftover oatmeal, buttermilk, crusts of bread. The only thing it would not eat was meat. Sometimes, if I accidentally gave the monster meat, it carefully left even the tiniest morsel untouched."

Koby raised his eyes from the book and looked at Mimi and Halley meaningfully.

"Eats no meat at all," Koby said. The girls nodded. Koby went on reading.

"The monster had an enormous appetite. Almost never did I manage to give it more food than it could eat. A usual portion was about a bucket full of whatever, 3 to

5 times a day. The monster liked a drink of water every so often, sometimes straight from puddles, and even a high mud content did not seem to present a problem.

"But over the weeks I noticed that the dust layer on its coat was growing thinner. Its color was turning lighter, actually fading and becoming dull. One could say with good reason that the monster was turning into a shadow or a ghost of its former self.

"As is commonly known, with animals as with humans, this is often a sign of an incorrectly balanced diet. This made me think that it could mean the same with monsters. In my heart I knew what I had to do: move with it into the nearby forest, its natural habitat. I hesitated for some time, as the risks were considerable.

"I took with me shiny green pieces of glass and a handheld silver mirror, items of which it was very fond. I knew it would come to me at any time, as long as it could see these objects that were so dear to it — "

"Now jump to the bit where it eats," Mimi interrupted. "I can remember this bit. Next they walk across the forest, the monster almost escapes, but Runar shows it the bits of glass and the mirror, and the monster runs back."

"Then they come to a dense thicket where it smells of rotted leaves, and the monster goes quite crazy with joy," Halley continued, yawning. It was getting very, very late.

Koby turned a few pages and went on reading.

"I soon realized that the source of the monster's joy was above all else the partly rotted leaves that had accumulated on the ground, which to any human would have been most repulsive as nutrition.

"The monster threw itself into this slimy, black, and earthy leaf mass, using both hands to gorge on it. It ate a large area of the ground as clean as a whistle. And that was not all. Having filled its belly, and belching loudly, the monster flung itself on the ground to wallow and roll around like a pig, and with great grunting and murring it rubbed as much of the stink of rotten leaves onto itself as it could. Then it simply fell asleep where it was, and I had no option but to sit down with my bits of glass to wait for it to wake up."

Koby stopped reading and looked at the girls.

"Do you want me to read the bit where it eats an anthill and falls asleep again? And where they find half-rotted fish on the beach and the monster gets excited, rubs them on its coat, and falls asleep once more? And the bit where—"

Mimi shook her head. "No need."

"Have you noticed that it falls asleep whenever it's eaten a bellyful?" Halley said. "And sleeps for hours? I wish it would sleep for hours now."

"The bathrobe said that monsters never sleep. And anyway, it's had nothing to eat today," Mimi said quietly.

"Although it should have had at least three buckets full of rotted leaves or anthills and such. It's probably awake in the hall closet and really hungry."

Halley said nothing. Koby was looking sternly at the book, frowning.

"How should we feed it? It said on that paper that it takes care of its own food. But how can it take care of its food if it's in that closet all the time?" he said.

"That book is useless," Halley snapped. "Only total idiots believe what they read in books!"

"Shut up," Koby snapped back. "If it weren't for this book, you wouldn't even know that the monster doesn't want to eat you."

"Surely nobody would send a monster to work as a nanny if it ate children, stupid," Halley pointed out.

"How can you be so sure?" Koby muttered ominously.

"Perhaps we should open the closet door and tell it to go out to the yard to eat," Mimi suggested. Halley and Koby kept silent.

"We could try it," Koby said. "Runar talked to his monster too. It wasn't dangerous. Let's turn on all the lights and go together. We'll knock on the closet door. We'll be real friendly and calm. Come on, let's go."

The children hesitantly got out of bed.

"Lights," Koby said, and turned on all the lights in their bedroom. They opened the door to the gloomy hall.

"Shall we put them all on?" Halley asked, and Mimi

nodded. They went around the whole apartment and switched on every light in every room. Light brought safety.

"Back to the hall," Halley said.

The children stood outside the monster's closet door, hesitating.

"Should we knock?" Mimi asked.

"Perhaps. I suppose it's polite," Koby said. "And the monster could be sleeping."

"It's not sleeping," Mimi repeated.

The children kept looking at one another for safety.

"Who'll knock?" Halley asked. Nobody answered.

"Who?" Halley repeated.

"You do it," Mimi suggested.

"Why?" Halley asked.

"You're the eldest," Mimi said.

"But I'm not talking to it," Halley said.

"I can do the talking," Mimi said.

"You?" Koby asked doubtfully. "Why?"

"I'm good at talking," Mimi said.

Koby and Halley exchanged looks.

"Very well. What are you going to say to it?" Halley asked.

"Nothing. I'll knock and listen," Mimi said.

"You are so weird," Halley told her, but raised her hand and, after a few seconds' hesitation, knocked. *Knock, knock, knock.*

In the dead silence of the night, the knocking sounded grim and ghostly. Nothing happened. The door stayed shut. It was very quiet.

"Perhaps it didn't hear," Koby whispered.

Halley raised her hand and knocked again, a little bolder and louder. *Knock, knock, knock!*

Then things started happening. There was a loud bang in the closet. The door flew open as if it had been kicked. Why would anyone kick the door open like that? Because they were seething with rage and meant to attack the knockers right away, of course. And possibly, despite all that stuff about not eating humans, would gobble them up, meat, bones, book, and all. The children screamed. Halley grabbed Mimi in her arms and jumped to one side. Koby lifted the big monster book to shield himself and closed his eyes. Yes, he was stupid to close his eyes, but sometimes one does senseless things when frightened.

Silence. Nobody rushed out of the closet. Koby opened his eyes and lowered the book. Halley took a step back and peeked inside. Mimi lifted her head, which she had pressed tightly against Halley's shoulder.

In the dark closet stood the monster, looking at them. Its scarily glowing yellow eyes ogled the children without expression.

"It was startled," Mimi said. "It got as big a fright as we did."

"What was that bang?" Koby asked.

The monster gazed at them. Then it raised one of its huge hands, slowly and hesitantly, and pointed at the left-hand wall and murred quietly. The children looked inside.

"What's that?" Halley asked.

On the wall, where the shelves had been, hung dark shreds.

"Oh, the poor thing!" Mimi exclaimed. "It got caught on the shelf hooks! Can you see, bits of its coat are hanging from them. Did you get hurt, monster?" The monster grunted and patted its upper arm clumsily.

"We startled it," Mimi said again. She reached out and carefully stroked the monster. When her hand touched its coat, a little cloud of monster dust puffed into the air.

"Mimi," Halley warned, alarmed.

"The monster really is kind. Just look at its eyes. It's really nice," Mimi said, stroking the monster. Halley and Koby looked at the monster's wild yellow eyes darting here and there.

In what way nice? The monster murred. Was it happy murring or dangerous human-eating murring? How could one tell? Koby and Halley gave each other an uncertain look.

"Mimi," Koby said in a low voice. "About the eating. Remember?"

Mimi nodded.

"Listen, monster," Mimi said slowly, looking directly

into the monster's wild eyes. "Are you hungry? We'd like you to eat something."

The monster glanced at the children furtively. Its eyes rolled from side to side. Then its gaze stopped on Mimi and it nodded clumsily. Koby and Halley drew breath. It understood speech!

"Good, very good," Mimi went on soothingly. "You eat old leaves and such, don't you? All sorts of things you find on the ground?"

The monster stared at Mimi with its tennis ball eyes. Then it started to nod and grunt excitedly.

"It's absolutely starving," Mimi explained to Koby and Halley, shaking her head with concern. "We've got to let it out to eat right now."

Mimi turned to the monster again.

"Come. We'll open the door for you. You can go find food for yourself. Look for whatever you want. There's a forest right behind the building."

The monster was watching Mimi. It was now perfectly still and quiet.

"Well, come on."

The monster slowly shook its head.

"What? Why won't you come?" Mimi asked.

The monster raised it big clumsy hand and pointed first at itself, then at Mimi, Koby, and Halley.

"What does it mean?" Koby asked.

"What do you mean, monster?" Mimi asked. The monster did the same motions again: the huge, fuzzy, dust-dropping hand rose slowly, pointed first at the monster itself, then at each child in turn. Then it seemed to hesitate for a moment, before raising its hand a little bit more and pointing at the front door.

"It wants us to go with it," Mimi said quietly.

"Why?" Koby asked.

"Well, I'm not going out to the forest in the middle of the night with a monster," Halley protested.

"Halley!" said Mimi, disapproving. "Just think how the monster feels. It's all alone in a strange place, it's starving hungry, and it got caught on the hooks on the closet wall. And then it's told it has to go outside alone to look for food. Just think if someone said that to you."

"I'm not a monster," Halley replied meaningfully.

"Bah! And you don't understand anything," Mimi huffed.

"Do you want us to come outside with you?" Koby asked the monster.

The monster turned to look at Koby and nodded slowly. Mimi had been right.

"Let's go, then," Koby said. "Come on, monster. We'll take you to the forest. Just behave yourself and don't frighten anybody."

The monster grunted and edged out of its cramped closet, dust flying from its coat.

CHAPTER 6

In the Forest

THE NIGHT FOREST WAS coolly damp and filled with all kinds of rustling. The sky was light and dusky at the same time, and a few ragged clouds wandered along, blown by the night wind.

"It's twelve fifty-two," Koby whispered, and pulled his sweater tighter around him.

"Is that late?" Mimi asked.

"Yes," Koby said. "You've never been out this late."

Mimi looked happy.

Halley's eyes darted around nervously. There were moving shadows and dark nooks all around, which could be hiding monsters or absolutely anything.

Their own monster was running around somewhere in the woods. It had disappeared as soon as they got to the back of the building and the edge of the forest. The monster, which indoors had seemed to be clumsy, had become sure-footed and nimble as soon as it got outside. In a few seconds it had vanished, and the children had no idea where it was.

"We'll never find it again, and a good thing, too," Halley said with a sniff.

"It'll come back, all right," Koby replied. "It has to take care of us."

"It won't come back," Halley insisted.

"Who'll look after us if the monster runs off?" Mimi asked.

"I will, of course. You didn't really believe that some monster would look after you?" Halley snapped. Koby and Mimi didn't answer. Koby's inquiring eyes scanned the forest.

"It'll come back. We'll just wait," he said evenly.

"No, it won't. I want to go home," Halley demanded. "It's cold and scary here. Let's go."

"We can't leave the monster here alone," Mimi said.

"Let's wait a bit. It'll be back soon," Koby said.

"I'm sleepy," Halley muttered.

"So am I," said Koby. "But it can't be helped now."

Halley sighed. "Let's at least walk a little, so it's not so cold."

"Okay, we'll walk," Koby agreed.

Near them ran a narrow path leading deeper into the forest. The children started walking. The path was so narrow that they had to walk single file. Koby was first, then Mimi, and Halley was last. Dense willows grew on both sides of the path, and their branches reached out toward them.

"It was the world's stupidest idea to bring that bathrobe along," Halley scolded Mimi, trying to dodge the branches. "I hope you drop it and never find it again."

Mimi didn't bother to answer. She had put the bathrobe on because Mom wasn't there to stop her. Mom never let her go out of the house in her bathrobe. But now everything was different. Mom wasn't home. It was after midnight. Mimi could wear her bathrobe if she wanted. And in any case, it wasn't worth answering Halley when she was in this mood. Halley only wanted to argue, and it had nothing to do with Mimi's bathrobe. It was all because Halley was cold and sleepy and scared. That would make anyone bad-tempered.

Suddenly Mimi stopped so quickly that Halley bumped into her.

"Ouch!" Halley yelped.

"Shhh," whispered Mimi.

The children froze on the spot. The translucent, light-dusky night enveloped them like mist.

"What did you hear?" Koby asked in a low voice.

"No, smell," Mimi whispered. "Smell the air. The monster is someplace very close."

Koby and Halley sniffed. From somewhere nearby came the familiar smell of earth cellar and rotten potato.

"Someone's compost stinks," Halley muttered, but Mimi and Koby paid no attention to her.

"Did you hear that!" Mimi asked suddenly. She turned her head from side to side, as if to hear better.

"What?" Koby whispered.

"Shhh," Mimi hissed.

The sound was tiny, just the kind you wouldn't have noticed in daylight. But in the silent summer's night, it was clearly discernible: something big and heavy was rolling on the ground and murring. Koby and Mimi exchanged a look.

"Our monster," Mimi said.

"Or a bear or wolf or moose," Halley whispered fearfully.

"That's the monster. And it must have eaten enough, because now it's rolling in the leaves just like in Runar's book. It'll fall asleep next," Koby said.

"Monsters do not sleep," Mimi corrected him.

"According to the book they do," Koby said. "In any case, if it's not asleep, why does it lie down motionless with its eyes closed? If it's not sleeping, what is it doing?"

"I can ask the bathrobe next time," Mimi replied.

Halley groaned silently but followed the others toward the sound. She didn't want to be left alone.

Silently creeping, the children pushed through the dense willows to the edge of a small clearing.

"Look," Koby whispered.

At the other side of the clearing, a big black creature was rolling and thrashing around. It had flung itself onto the ground; it spun and wallowed. It almost looked as if it were trying to swim. Or hug the ground. The stench of rotted leaves filled the clearing.

"It's happy," Mimi whispered. "Look how it rolls and murs."

Halley shook her head in disbelief. There was their nanny thrashing around. Their own house monster.

The air was thick with monster dust, and more puffed off the monster as it rolled around. The light wind blew the dust toward the children, and a few specks of it drifted straight into Halley's nose. And since Halley's nose was already irritated, it instantly started to want to sneeze quite uncontrollably. Nothing could be done about it. Halley sneezed, and in the silent summer night, the sneeze sounded pretty much the same as a cannon shot. Mimi let out a scream in fright. Koby jumped. A few birds that had been asleep flapped into the air, startled.

Naturally, the sneeze was also heard by the monster, and it stopped rolling. It froze on the spot and listened. How well can monsters hear? The children had not yet read that bit in Runar's book.

The monster stood up slowly and turned its yellow glowing eyes toward the children.

"Can it see us?" Halley asked, frightened.

"Perhaps," Koby whispered.

"Monster! Here we are! Here!" yelled Mimi, waving her arm.

"Are you crazy!" Halley hissed, and pushed Mimi's arm down.

"What do you mean? It's our monster. Didn't we come looking for it?" Mimi asked, puzzled.

On the other side of the clearing, the monster shook its coat and started padding toward them. The ground thumped with the weight of its steps, and with every one, its ragged coat shed leaves, twigs, and clumps of earth. The monster looked as if it had grown in height and girth. It looked magnificent and powerful.

"Look how beautiful it is," Mimi said, sighing adoringly. Koby and Halley didn't answer. The monster coming toward them in the summer night had left them dumbfounded.

The monster stopped in front of them. Its eyes had a new wild glow as it looked at the children.

"Feeling better now?" Mimi asked. "Had enough to eat?" The monster grunted and slapped its belly. Mimi giggled.

"Shall we go home now?" she asked.

The monster nodded. It bent down a little as if to get

set and then charged straight through the thicket. The air filled with crashing and snapping as branches cracked and broke off. The monster growled as it went, but it sounded contented. It was good, strong monster growling.

"Wait for us!" Mimi shouted, and set off running after the monster. It was easy to run through the bushes now. The monster had made a big opening in them, almost like a gate.

"Come on, come on!" Mimi called to Halley and Koby. "Monster! Wait a minute!"

Farther away in the gloomy forest, the monster stopped and grunted hollowly like a huge pig.

"You run really fast," Mimi complimented it when they caught up to the monster. "You'll have to move a little slower now, or nobody will be able to keep up with you."

"Speak for yourself, Mimi," muttered Halley, who had been the winner at least twice in school running races. If Mimi couldn't keep up with the monster, it didn't mean that Halley couldn't.

"You're no match for the monster," Mimi giggled. "Or do you want to try?"

It was a question that should have been left unasked. Because there were some things that Halley could not resist. Things like chocolate, soccer, and a new baseball cap for her collection. They were all important things in Halley's life, but they were nothing compared to what she was really interested in: competing. Any kind of competing. The mere thought of a competition filled Halley with irresistible euphoria and buzzing that whooshed right up to her ears.

"Let's have a race, monster!" Halley said defiantly. This was the first time she spoke to the monster directly.

The monster looked at Mimi. Was it asking for permission?

"Take no notice. Halley is like that. She always wants to race," Mimi said to the monster, and wrinkled her nose.

"Halley, it's not worth racing with the monster," Koby said. "You saw how it charged through the trees. It's incredibly strong."

Halley rolled her eyes at Koby. "But I'm fast," she said. "I don't need to go through trees."

"Of course you're fast, but do you see, the monster is a thousand times faster."

"We'll race and then we'll know," Halley insisted, throwing a challenging look at the monster.

The monster was still staring at Mimi, who let out a sigh. There was no stopping Halley.

"Run, if you want to," Mimi said to the monster.

The monster grunted and held out its earthy, dark hand to Mimi, who took it right away. How tiny Mimi's hand looked on the monster's palm! Almost as if the monster were holding a lollipop or a little goldfish in its hand.

The monster bent down and lightly picked Mimi up in its arms. Mimi sneezed.

"Awful dust. We'll have to take you out to the rug-beating rack to give you a bashing," Mimi giggled.

The monster murred happily.

"It likes Mimi," Koby said to Halley. "Don't you think?"

But Halley didn't hear. She was excited by the thrill of the race and eyed the monster boldly.

"Are you going to run while carrying Mimi?" Halley asked. The monster turned to Halley and nodded.

"Very well," Halley said. "But you're counted as one runner. The finish line is our door. No tricks. Nothing like throwing Mimi through the forest. We're going to run—do you understand? The winner is whoever first touches their foot to the front door of our building."

The monster nodded. Mimi was sneezing and giggling in its arms.

"What about me?" Koby asked.

"Follow us," Halley replied haughtily. She always became a little bit boastful at sporting contests. Koby was not a particularly fast runner.

"I don't want to be left alone in the forest. Having a race is really stupid," Koby said.

"What, you're not scared, are you?" Halley sniggered.

"You are such a numskull, Halley," Mimi said, sneezing. "Monster, can you pick up Koby, too?"

"N—" Koby started before the monster scooped him up in its other arm.

"*Achoo!* I'm not—*Achoo!*—sure if I want—*Achoo!*"

"Be quiet for once," Mimi giggled, then sneezed. "We'll beat Halley easily. She hasn't got a hope. *Achoo!*"

"Ready, set, GO!" Halley yelled, and raced off in the direction of home as fast as her legs would carry her.

"False start!" Koby shouted, but he had no time to say anything more, as the monster shot off after Halley. Koby quickly closed his mouth and eyes. The less one knew about the scenery flashing by, the less scared one was.

The monster did not dodge tree stumps or trees or anything at all. It stormed ahead like a hippopotamus or a steam engine. Its huge heart beat hollowly deep inside its chest. The monster murred and grunted, one hoped more with contentment than rage, but one could not be absolutely sure. Tree branches swiped at Koby and Mimi, and they yelped quietly. It was impossible to avoid scratches in the monster's arms. On the other hand, such speed could not be experienced anywhere else. It felt like they were on a roller coaster that only went downhill.

Until, that is, the monster stopped dead. The stop was so sudden and unexpected that it was only the monster's thick arms that kept Mimi and Koby from being flung into the bushes. Silence hissed in their ears. The monster's heart thumped in its chest; apart from that, it was totally quiet.

Koby and Mimi opened their eyes, frightened. They were not at home yet. They were in a very dense thicket near the building. The monster's alert, wild eyes stared through the bushes toward the other side.

"Achoo." Mimi sneezed as quietly as she could and pressed her face against the

monster's chest. Of course, that was a mistake, as she only wanted to sneeze more than ever.

"Achoo, achoo, achoo!" Mimi sneezed in a muffled voice.

The sound was not much, but it was enough. Somewhere very close, a dog started to bark angrily, almost accusingly.

Mimi got such a fright that she stopped sneezing instantly. She knew the barker. It was Eric from the first floor, the most fearsome dog in the world. He was a dog who wanted to know everything and poke his nose into everything. He was a dog who thought himself the official guard of the apartment building and therefore raised a horrendous racket if anything unusual happened. And there was no doubt that running through the forest at night with a monster was unusual. Eric was barking like crazy. They could only hope that he was on his leash.

"Eric, what's the matter? That's enough—you'll wake everyone up," a voice said very close, on the other side of the bush. Mimi's heart missed a beat. It was Eric's owner, Pattie Newhouse. Eric yapped and ranted; the whole summer night was filled with his barking.

"Eric! Enough!" the lady scolded. "What is it, anyway? A mole? Want to go and see?"

Mimi stopped breathing with sheer terror. What if Mrs. Newhouse let Eric off his leash? What do monsters do to yapping dogs? And yapping dogs to monsters?

Suddenly there was a sound of cracking and huffing from the forest. Halley! She had picked what she thought was a clever shortcut to the door.

Eric was confused and pricked up his ears. Judging by the sound, Halley was approaching fast. She was so enthralled by the race that she didn't see Eric until she leapt out of the bushes right in front of him and fell over the dog.

"Good grief!" Mrs. Newhouse shrieked.

"Woof-woof-woof-woof-woof!" barked Eric, as startled as his owner.

"Ouch!" yelped Halley, grabbing her knee. The gravel on the yard path bit straight through the thin pajama bottoms into her skin.

"Halley, isn't it? Halley Hellman?" the lady rambled. "What are you doing, running around in the middle of the night? Shouldn't you be in bed?"

Halley rubbed her knee and thought feverishly. Mimi and Koby knew that right now, Halley, the fastest girl in the school and possibly the whole town, would have given anything to be able to borrow Koby's or Mimi's head for a moment. Halley didn't know what she should say. She couldn't say anything about the monster; the instructions said so. But she had to say something. Give some kind of explanation for why she was out alone in the middle of the night. Something believable but not too revealing.

"Halley?" Mrs. Newhouse repeated, concerned. Eric

had calmed down and bent down to sniff Halley. "Halley? What is it? Are you all right? Where is your mother?"

Halley slowly lifted her head and looked around with exaggerated surprise. "What? Where am I?" she asked in a sleepy voice. "Mom?"

Mrs. Newhouse bent down to Halley and gently shook her by the shoulders.

"Halley, should I call an ambulance?" she asked. "Are you sick?"

Halley's performance really was a little ghostly. Only Mimi on the other side of the bushes knew what was coming. This was not the first time Halley had pretended to be sleepwalking.

Last Christmas, Mom had hidden the Christmas chocolates in a big tin in a top cupboard in the kitchen. Halley had found the hiding place and sneaked in to steal some chocolate a couple of times before Christmas. On the third night, Halley had asked Mimi to go with her. Unfortunately, Mom had begun to suspect something. She had stayed in the kitchen to wait. Halley and Mimi had tiptoed to the kitchen door, Halley first. At the door Halley had spotted Mom. It was too late to back off, because Mom had already seen Halley. So Halley had done the same as now: pretended to be sleepwalking in such an amazingly strange way that to this day Mom didn't know that it was all a sham. Halley hardly ever shammed. She was feisty and reliable. But even she had her weaknesses, one of them being chocolate.

"She'll wake up soon. It's really weird. Looks like some kind of an attack," Mimi whispered to Koby and the monster.

"Wake up?" Koby repeated.

Halley began to jerk and twitch. Then she jumped to her feet, horrified, and yelled dramatically:

"Where am I? Where's my bed?"

"What are you saying?" Mrs. Newhouse asked, surprised. Eric let out a baffled bark.

Halley's eyes darted about as if she had never seen this very bush in her yard.

"Oh no, it's happened again!" she wailed.

"What's happened?" the lady asked, worried. Even Eric was quiet and watching Halley quizzically.

"I walked in my sleep again! This must end." Halley almost sobbed. She was very believable. "I'm going to see the doctor tomorrow. Mom can take me."

Koby shook his head in the bush. He was afraid that Halley's performance was going too far.

"Don't worry," Mimi whispered. "She's doing fine."

"So you were sleepwalking," Mrs. Newhouse said doubtfully. "You're not hurt or anything? I think you were in the woods."

Halley looked at the forest, horrified. "Alone in the

forest? I want to go home to my mommy now. To my sister and brother! And that smelly mo . . . mo . . ."

Halley stopped, startled. How could she be so stupid? In the bush, Koby and Mimi were holding their breath and thinking the same. But Halley was not stupid. Her brain kept ticking away, and she thought of a rescue route.

"Mollycuddle!" she spat out, and sighed with relief.

"Mollycuddle?" the lady repeated, puzzled.

"Yes. My teddy bear," Halley explained, agitated. "I'll go now. Thank you for waking me. I'll put the safety chain on tomorrow night."

"You should always have the safety chain on," the lady advised her, but Halley was already rushing toward the door.

For a moment it looked like Halley was going to run straight inside, but just before the front door she stopped and let her eyes scan all the shadowy bushes. Then, slowly and deliberately, she raised her foot and touched the bottom of the door with it. If you happened to have a monster's ears, you clearly would have heard her whisper triumphantly: "First at the door. I win."

Then Halley slipped inside. Mrs. Newhouse watched her go.

"Shall we go in too, Eric?" she chatted to the dog, and tugged his leash. "Come along, doggy-bobs."

But the monster, Koby, and Mimi waited behind the bush for a long time yet. The monster would not move an inch. Maybe it had gotten too frightened. Or maybe it was just listening to the night, all the crackles and trees sighing, night birds twittering, Koby and Mimi awkwardly sneezing in its arms. Maybe it liked night and didn't want to go inside yet.

Only when the lights went out in the first-floor windows, Eric's home, did the monster move. It murred quietly and took a cautious step. It knew how to move quite noiselessly, lightly, like a moth. In the shadows, they sneaked to the main door. They slipped into the building, over to the elevator, and up to the fifth floor, and just as noiselessly into their home.

Halley sat waiting for them on the hall rug, wrapped up in her duvet. Not because she was cold, but because she was scared. When Halley was scared, she always wanted to wrap up in her duvet.

"Where did you get to?" Halley asked weepily.

Koby and Mimi crouched down next to Halley on the mud mat and hugged her. The monster took a few hesitant, dust-shedding and dirt-clump-dropping steps toward the children, bent over clumsily, and hugged all three of them very gently and tenderly.

CHAPTER 7

Mimi Talks to the Monster

THE SUN WAS SHINING high in the summer sky straight through the window at Mimi's nose. Mimi sneezed.

It was a sun sneeze, not a monster sneeze, but Mimi woke up at once. She looked around her.

She was lying on a mattress on the living room floor. They had carried everybody's mattresses into the living room, because they had wanted to sleep near each other. Not that they were scared. If you've run with a monster in the forest after midnight, you are not scared of monsters anymore. But it was strange to be at home without Mom. It felt best for them all to sleep next to one another. Indeed: all of them. Because on Mimi's right-hand side lolled the monster. It lay on its back on the floor, looking at the ceiling, its great dark chest rising and falling.

"Hey, monster," Mimi whispered.

The monster turned its yellow eyes to Mimi and grunted.

"Good morning," Mimi said, smiling. "Have you noticed, I'm not sneezing anymore. I've gotten used to you."

The monster said nothing, just watched.

"Do you ever sleep at all?" Mimi asked. The monster

didn't answer. In the hopeful, happy rays of the morning sun, the monster looked like a giant teddy bear that had been dropped in a muddy puddle.

"Listen, where did you come from?" Mimi asked. The monster turned its gaze to the ceiling, but Mimi wouldn't give up.

"Have you got a mom or dad? How old are you? Where did you live before you came here?"

The monster stared at the ceiling.

"Strange that you don't have a name," Mimi went on. "Can I give you a name? I've given names to at least fifty stuffed animals. Really! Megan would suit you, perhaps. Or Richard, if you're a boy. No, I know: Firefast. You are so fast."

The monster shifted restlessly. It turned toward Mimi and grunted: "Grah."

"Firefast is good, don't you think?" Mimi said, pleased. The monster rolled its eyes.

"Grah," it growled emphatically. "Grah."

"Grah," Mimi repeated. "What does it mean? Do you have your own language? Can you talk? Can I learn that language?"

The monster eyed Mimi and echoed, "Grah."

"Grah," Mimi said.

The monster slowly raised its big hand and touched its chest. "Grah."

"Is that your name? Grah?" Mimi asked, surprised.

The monster nodded.

Mimi quickly sat up and tugged the covers off Koby and Halley.

"Wake up—our monster has a name!" Mimi said hurriedly. "Did you hear? It's called Grah."

The monster grabbed Mimi's arm.

"Let's wake them up! They'll be so pleased, I'm sure," Mimi gabbled happily. "Grah suits you really well. By the way, are you a boy or a girl?"

The monster shook its head and hissed.

"What?" Mimi asked, confused.

The monster put its thick finger in front of its mouth and hissed again.

"You're not allowed to tell?" Mimi asked. The monster shook its head.

"Why not? It's a really good name."

The monster clambered up with difficulty and disappeared into the hall. It returned holding the crumpled instruction sheet, which it handed to Mimi.

"I can't read," Mimi said. "This is that note of yours. Why did you bring it to me?"

Grah stirred restlessly. It raised its finger to its mouth again and hissed. The gesture did not look natural, but the monster clearly knew what it meant. Mimi frowned.

Halley raised her head, annoyed.

"What's all the racket?" she grumbled. "Turn off the lights. I want to sleep."

"It's the sun; it can't be turned off," Mimi answered. "Halley, please wake up."

"No," mumbled Halley, and pulled her duvet over her head.

"Koby?" Mimi said cautiously.

The monster's finger went up to its mouth again.

"Don't worry, Grah. We're friends. We'll help you, really we will," Mimi tried to reassure it. "We won't tell anyone."

The monster glanced at Koby and rolled its eyes.

"We have to tell Koby," Mimi whispered. "Koby can read in that monster book . . ."

Mimi fell silent and watched the monster. Maybe it wasn't happy about the children having a book on monsters? Grah stared at Mimi with its glowing eyes.

"We've got a book that tells all about monsters. Would you like to see it?" Mimi asked.

Grah made no reply.

Mimi jumped up off the mattress and ran into their bedroom. She knew where Koby had hidden the book: in the toy box under the bed. She ran back into the living room, book under her arm.

"Here, look. It's about a monster. But I can't read. We'll have to wake Koby so he can read it to you."

The monster took the book carefully. How small and fragile it looked in the monster's gigantic hairy hands!

Those fingers were unlikely to turn the pages without tearing them to shreds. And that would make Koby cross.

"Let me help," Mimi said quickly, and took the book from the monster's lap.

Mimi leafed through the book and finally found Runar's pencil drawings. They were not particularly good drawings but were recognizable as monsters anyway.

"Look, here are some pictures of that monster. It looks like you, but one of its ears is a bit ragged. Maybe it's been in some sort of an accident. I think it looks a lot older than you. It's quite pale gray."

Grah made a strange noise and snatched the book from Mimi's hand.

"Careful," Mimi whispered apprehensively, and glanced at the sleeping Koby. "It's a library book. It's really, really important to Koby."

The monster gently brought the book right up to its face. It studied Runar's drawings, humming quietly.

"That's the monster the book's writer found in a forest. I don't know what its name was. It must have gone back to its home," Mimi chattered. Grah sat perfectly still, its eyes glued to the book.

Monsters have a strange habit of becoming motionless, Mimi thought. The monster could be as still as a sofa or kitchen table. Then it became almost impossible to see. It blended with its background, regardless of where it was.

"Grah," Mimi whispered, and stroked the monster's furry arm. A dust cloud puffed up in the air. In the sunshine it looked like a swarm of jellyfish floating in the ocean.

The monster behind the dust seemed to have come to life. It grunted once; then it grunted again. The third grunt became a roar that rattled the windows. Halley and Koby sprang up with fright.

"What's happening!" Halley shrieked.

The monster grunted for a fourth time, now very quietly. The book fell from its grip as it put its hands to its face and started croaking and groaning.

"Is it crying?" Halley asked. "What's the matter with it? Why did it roar?"

"Why did it have the monster book?" Koby asked Mimi. "Did you give it the monster book, dummy?"

"You're the dummy!" Mimi yelled, alarmed. "You wouldn't wake up, even though I tried to wake you! And why shouldn't I show it that book? Of course I can! You read books about people, you know!"

"It's a monster—that's the difference," Koby mumbled. "Probably can't even read. Its fingers are so big, it could tear the book to bits quite by accident."

"No, it couldn't! And anyway, its name is not monster; it's Grah. It told me itself," Mimi declared.

The monster croaked and spluttered, hands over its eyes. Its matted shoulders shook.

"Stop yelling," Halley said. "Look, it's crying."

Enormous, mud-water gray tears were oozing from between the monster's fingers, running down its arms, and vanishing somewhere inside its coat.

Mimi and Koby went quiet.

"Why are you crying, Grah?" Mimi asked.

"Who?" Halley said.

"Apparently that's its name," Koby said.

"How do you know?" Halley asked.

"It told me itself," Mimi snapped. "Maybe it would tell you, too, if you occasionally bothered to listen. And just look, the whole floor is soaking!"

Halley and Koby looked at the floor. The puddle was

growing as they watched. The tears were now running in small under-fur rivulets straight onto the floor.

"Get some towels, quickly!" Mimi commanded.

Halley and Koby ran to the linen closet.

One towel wasn't enough. The monster wept, grunted, and shook. More and more tears came.

"Why are you crying?" Mimi asked, stroking the monster's arm. The monster didn't answer.

"How did it tell you its name? What is it, again?" Halley inquired as she spread a towel on the floor.

"Whatever gave you the idea to show it the book?" Koby demanded, drying the puddle at the monster's feet. (Very dirty feet indeed, he noted.) "I hope the pages aren't ripped. I bet the whole book is gray with dust."

Koby put the sopping wet towel into a bucket, which they had carried into the living room.

Mimi did not reply. She looked at Grah and asked gently: "Why are you crying, Grah?"

Grah lifted its watery eyes, gray from the tears, to Mimi. The monster moaned quietly and then pointed at the book lying on the floor, at a safe distance.

"Do you want that book?" Mimi asked.

"No!" Koby called out.

Grah nodded, and Mimi glanced at Koby.

"How about if I just hold it?" she suggested. Koby sighed.

Mimi opened the book to the drawings and lifted it close to the monster's eyes. Halley and Koby stopped drying the floor and watched the monster. It was not crying anymore, just moaning quietly and staring at the drawings.

"Is it someone you know?" Mimi asked. Her arms were starting to ache from the weight of the book. It was a very heavy book.

Grah moaned quietly, eyes fixed on the pictures.

"Mimi, sometimes you are really sharp," Koby said admiringly.

Mimi turned to Koby, surprised.

"Well, I suppose I am quite clever. The bathrobe wouldn't talk to me if I weren't," she replied kindly.

"Aww! Don't keep going on about that stupid bathrobe!" Halley spat out.

Mimi paid no attention to Halley. She was well used

to her and her anti-bathrobe attitude. She would rather focus on the monster.

"Is it one of your friends?" Mimi asked.

The monster shook its head and wailed.

"Is it your mother or father?" Mimi went on.

The monster shook its head sadly.

"Your . . . cousin? Or neighbor? Or classmate?" Mimi continued, but the monster just shook its head. Mimi appealed to Halley and Koby with a look. Who else could it be in the pictures?

"Your pen pal?" Mimi asked. "Or soccer teammate?"

"Soccer teammate," Koby repeated. "Really, Mimi."

"How do we know what a monster's life is like?" Mimi said, and turned back to Grah: "Is it your work colleague?"

The monster shook its head. Then it raised its hand and patted its chest.

"Grah," it grunted. "Grah-ih-Gru."

"Yes, yes, your name is Grah, we know. But who is that in the picture?" Mimi spoke to it kindly.

The monster looked at the children miserably and tapped its chest again. Then it pointed at the book. It was very quiet. Mimi couldn't think of any others who might be in the picture.

"Just a minute," Halley said suddenly. "Could it be . . . Grah, is that you in the picture?"

Grah shook its head. "Grah," it again repeated quietly,

and touched its chest. "Grah-ih-Gru," it then said, and pointed at the book.

"It's some Grah-ih-something," Halley said.

"Is that some Grah-ih-what's-his-name?" Mimi asked the monster.

The monster covered its face with its hands and began to sob again, shoulders shaking. Mimi kept stroking its big, dark, dust-shedding shoulders.

"We need more towels," Halley said.

"There, there now," Mimi said, trying to soothe the monster. "That's grand, that it's Grah-ih-something. Someone you know is in Runar's book. Very nice."

The monster wept three more towels full before it stopped. Koby and Halley mopped up the last pools of water off the floor and dumped the towels in the shower. The towels were gray and grimy, as if they had been used to mop up the garden.

"It must be thirsty," Halley guessed, looking at the soaked towels. "It's cried several buckets full of water."

"We'll have to take it outside to drink from some ditch," Koby said. "But not until it's dark. To think that Grah knew that old monster. I wonder how many monsters there are? And we never knew a thing."

"We did have an idea. You were always scared of monsters," Halley said, grinning. Koby had always been pretty fearful at night. Koby threw a dirty towel at Halley, but her quick feet dodged it easily.

"Maybe there are monsters in other people's homes too," Halley said. "I think I'll go on a little expedition."

Koby agreed. "Do that."

"Hey," Mimi called from the living room. "Did you hear — there's a text message on the phone. Maybe it's from Mom. Go and see! The phone is on the kitchen table."

Koby and Halley ran into the kitchen, shoving each other. The phone was in the middle of the table among leftovers and dirty plates.

"Ugh," Halley groaned. "The monster sure isn't very good at cleaning up."

"Grah," Koby corrected her. "Its name is Grah."

He picked up the phone and opened the message. "It's from Mom," he confirmed.

"Come in here to read it. I can't move!" Mimi yelled from the living room.

"What do you mean you can't move?" Halley yelled back.

"I'm having a cuddle with the monster!" Mimi answered happily. "This is a real tight cuddle!"

"And you are quite dirty," Halley sniffed from the doorway.

Mimi looked like she had been caught in a gray sand-storm.

"Oh, never mind. What does Mom say?" Mimi asked, her cheek against the monster's shoulder.

Koby raised the phone and read:

"Dear children! Is
everything all right? Dad
has come, hasn't he?
Have you got food? Miss
you terribly!! Lapland
is beautiful. Breakfast
starts soon! Then I'll
know more about
the day's program.
Please write! How's the
monster? Miss you, miss
you!

"Love, Mom"

"OK, let's reply right away," Mimi said. "Dear Mom, waiting for Invisible Voice here. The monster is gorgeous! We were out with it last night. Nobody does any cleaning, and the monster cried many buckets of muddy water on the living room floor, but we mopped it up."

Koby and Halley exchanged glances.

"We can't write that," Koby said. "Mom's relaxation holiday would be ruined."

Mimi looked at them. "What, then?" she asked.

"This, for instance," Koby replied, and began to tap:

> "Hi, Mom! We miss you
> lots, too. All is well.
> Monster is nice and
> looks after us well . . ."

Halley eyed the monster, who was hugging Mimi. Koby went on writing: "So everything is OK."

"Don't keep saying that everything is OK. It sounds suspicious. Mom will guess that we're hiding something."

"Oh," Koby said, and deleted the last sentence. "What shall I put, then?"

Halley snatched the phone and continued with the writing:

> "We have done the
> cleaning. We have eaten
> healthy food at proper
> mealtimes. Broccoli, rye
> bread, and milk. Hope
> you are having fun! Dad
> has not come yet but will
> be here soon. Write to
> us again!"

"But we haven't done any cleaning or eaten broccoli," Koby began, but piped down when Halley raised her eyebrows meaningfully.

"Shall we tell her that the monster has a name?" Mimi suggested with a sneeze as the monster dust went up her nose.

The monster grunted and shook its head vehemently.

"*Achoo!* All right, all right," Mimi murmured.

"I'm sending this now," Halley said, and sent the message.

"Shall we have some breakfast?" Mimi proposed.

At that, the monster let go of Mimi and jumped up with surprising agility. It was a nanny monster, after all.

"And after breakfast, Halley will go and find out if there are monsters in any other homes," Koby said.

"I'm coming with you!" Mimi yelled, delighted.

"You so are not," Halley said.

"You can stay with me and Grah to read the monster book," Koby suggested, trying to keep the peace. "We'll wait for Invisible Voice. I'm sure he'll be here in a few hours."

Mimi sniffed and studied her gray arms. "No, I'm having a bath instead."

Koby and Halley exchanged a look.

"Good idea," Halley said.

CHAPTER 8

Detective at Work

HALLEY RANG OSCAR'S DOORBELL for a second time. The sound of the bell could be heard clearly through the door in the stairway. But there was no other sound. It was as quiet as a tomb. No sound of people talking, no footsteps. No background noise from a television. Where was everybody? Not just Oscar, but everyone else, too. Halley's friends, other people they knew vaguely. Where were they all? Was the whole apartment building empty?

Oscar's doorbell was not the first Halley had rung. Why would it be? Halley had never been to Oscar's home; she only knew where Oscar lived. They played in the school soccer club in wintertime and were in the same class—that was all. But Halley couldn't think of anybody else whose door she could try. She had already been to the doors of everybody she knew, absolutely everybody.

Halley pressed the doorbell for a third time. Silence fell in the stairway. Halley sighed and sat down on the stairs. The stairwell was empty and echoing; even the automatic lights would go out soon. Everybody had vanished. And their home would soon vanish in the gray monster dust.

The lights went out, but Halley didn't move. What did any of it actually matter? It was just as well to sit in a dark stairway in front of the door of some half-acquaintance. Halley closed her eyes. Inside her head, behind her eyelids, it was just as dark as in the stairway.

Suddenly there was a rustle. Little bumps, maybe footsteps. More rustling. An interior door was opened somewhere. Halley opened her eyes and turned toward Oscar's door. There was a cautious click, and Oscar's mail slot opened slowly. A weak streak of light escaped into the stairway.

"All dark," someone whispered. The voice was not a grownup voice. But it wasn't Oscar's voice either. "There's nobody here now. They've gone away."

Halley was baffled. Were they talking about her? Of course they were. Who else. But why didn't they want to open the door to her? How rude!

The mail slot closed with a slight *clack*. The talking was fainter now, but you could still make out what was being said. Halley smiled. Mom was right: you should keep the inner door closed if you wanted to tell secrets. Oscar's mom was not nearly as good an adviser as Halley's mom.

Halley got up quietly and carefully pushed open the mail slot.

"Did you see that? Someone opened the mail slot," a voice whispered, scared. It sounded like a young child, maybe Oscar's little sister.

"You left it open," someone explained dismissively.

"I did not," the first voice whispered. "Somebody's out there."

"A draft opened it," said Oscar's voice.

As soon as Halley heard Oscar's voice, she knew what to do. Oscar, the school scaredy-cat! Halley remembered one time when all the lights in the soccer club hall had gone out, and Oscar had been so scared that he had almost peed his pants. Especially after Halley had let out particularly frightening howls, just like a horrible, deadly cold ghost . . . Just like she intended to do again right now.

"*Woo . . . wooo-wooooo,*" Halley whispered in a voice from the grave into Oscar's mail slot.

Somebody let out a scream behind the door. Someone else began to cry. Halley felt a sting in her conscience. She heard Oscar's voice saying to the others: "Hey, wait, I've heard that voice before."

Oscar bent down to peek through the mail slot into the dark stairway. "Halley? Is that you?"

Infuriating! How could Oscar guess that it was her? She had sounded as much like a real ghost as anybody could sound.

"*Woooo . . . woooo . . .*" Halley howled again, so believably that even her own hair stood on end. There was a rustle and suddenly the door opened, much more quickly than Halley had expected.

"Ouch!" she yelled, holding her nose. "You hit my nose with the door!"

"That'll teach you to stand with your nose stuck in our door," Oscar said. "Quick, get in. You can explain to Alice yourself that you're not a ghost."

Halley slipped inside Oscar's home. The door closed behind her. It was almost dark; all the venetian blinds were closed. Next to Oscar stood a girl Halley had sometimes seen in the school yard. Someone else's alarmed crying came from a back room. Halley felt rotten.

"Alice, come and see. It's not a ghost, just a girl from our school," Oscar called. "Now look what you've done," he said to Halley, annoyed.

"Sorry," Halley said, and called toward the crying girl, "Alice, it was me! It was just a joke."

Then she turned back to Oscar and asked him accusingly: "Why didn't you answer the door?"

Oscar and the girl glanced at each other hesitantly. Alice's tearful face appeared in a doorway near the hall.

Halley gave her a friendly wave and turned back to Oscar. Something strange was afoot, that was for sure.

"Is your mom home?" she asked.

"No, she isn't," Oscar said. "Mom is . . ."

". . . at work, of course," the girl finished, and gave Oscar a meaningful look.

"Pity," Halley said, and thought for a moment. She needed a little more information before she could be sure.

"And your dad?"

"No, he's not either. Dad's at work too," Oscar went on, a little more naturally now.

"I'm really thirsty. Could I get some water from the kitchen?" Halley asked.

"I'll get it!" Oscar and the girl both shouted quickly.

"No, I can get it myself," Halley said calmly, watching their reaction.

"We can get it!" Oscar and the girl yelled too eagerly, almost desperately.

Oscar turned on his heel and ran off. Halley stayed in the hall with the girl, who seemed nervous.

"Do you live here too?" Halley asked.

"N-no," the girl answered.

"So where do you live?" Halley went on.

"Next door. We're neighbors. Oscar's mom and my mom go to Latin dancing together."

"Latin dancing," Halley repeated under her breath,

and shook her head. How different the world's moms were.

"It's true," the girl said defensively.

"Do you have sisters or brothers? Or a father?" Halley continued questioning.

"No. I mean, yes, but Mom and I live here just the two of us. Dad lives in another town," the girl replied.

Halley nodded. The situation was pretty clear. One more question.

"What's your name?"

"Minnie," the girl said.

"Oh, as in Minnie Mouse?" Halley asked.

The girl sniffed, irritated. "Well, no. It's a nickname. My real name is Minea."

Oscar ran into the hall, water spilling from a glass in his hand.

"Here you go," he said, out of breath. "Sorry it took so long, but all the dishes were dirty and I had to wash a glass."

Halley took the glass and sipped the water. She watched Minnie and Oscar. Then she looked at the walls. The apartment was so gloomy that you couldn't see the monster dust, if there was any.

"Why have you closed all the blinds?" she asked.

"What do you want?" Oscar asked nervously. "Why did you come?"

Halley took one more gulp from her glass of water.

Then she fixed her gaze on Oscar and Minnie and said: "I came to ask if you have a monster nanny here, too. You see, we have one."

Oscar froze to the spot, and Minnie took such a deep breath that she had a coughing fit.

"Here, drink some water," Halley said, handing Minnie the glass.

CHAPTER 9

The Monster's Nocturnal Habits

KOBY PICKED UP THE book off the floor and brushed the worst of the monster dust from its cover. *Monsters: Characteristics and Qualities of the Species in Light of My Experiences,* by Runar Kalli.

With the book under his arm, he walked into the bedroom and flopped onto the beanbag chair. He could hear Mimi's voice from the bathroom. She was having a discussion with her bathrobe again.

At that moment, Koby was not interested or even bothered. He had other things to do. He intended to study Runar Kalli's book, because they needed more information.

Koby opened the book and stroked its yellowed flyleaf. Runar had been a brave man. He had written his book despite knowing that nobody would believe a word of it.

Only now had the book found a reader who understood its worth. Koby scanned the table of contents, taking his time.

Halley may be right, he thought. In an emergency, it was sensible to read a book in many places at the same time. The idea felt odd, even a little reckless, but exceptional circumstances demanded exceptional measures. There were many things to which Koby wanted answers. For example: Why did the monster want to go into the closet to stand there, eyes closed, if it didn't sleep? Koby's eyes stopped at Chapter 5 of Part II ("Real Monsters"): "The Monster's Appearance and Characteristics."

Koby turned the pages until he got to the beginning of the chapter. He read:

> In appearance, monsters resemble humans to a surprising degree. Maybe this observation is shocking, as we do not want to believe that we have any connection with monsters and other legendary beings. However, the relationship is probably only distant, since there are also significant differences, as we will see later.
>
> The monster's body shape can be described as sturdy. The height of the monster I studied was six feet at the time of measuring, and its weight so amazingly great that my scale, going up to 300 pounds, was insufficient to weigh it.
>
> The monster's hands and feet are large. The foot is

rounded in shape, about 12 inches in diameter. There are four toes on the feet, and on each toe is a shortish, not very sharp nail. One could almost say a human-like nail, but bigger in size. The skin of the sole is very thick, and the monster does not appear to feel cold or pain through it.

The hands are almost as big as the feet, if measured from the tips of the thick, strong fingers. The fingers are all the same thickness and length, and there are four of them, too. It should be noted that the monster's fingers have one joint more than those of humans. The monster's joints also bend not only toward the palm, but also sideways. Thus, the monster's fingers bend strangely from the human point of view, resembling bendy monkey tails.

Koby lifted his head from the book. Monkey tails! Runar used unusual comparisons. Koby read on.

> The monster's head is large in relation to the rest of its body. The shape of the head is round. The strangest feature in the monster's face is its eyes. They are the size of apples and yellowish green in color. They roll and move from side to side at amazing speed. Their movements are not always simultaneous with each other. One might ask whether or not a monster can look in two different directions at the same time.
>
> The teeth are typical herbivore teeth . . .

Koby stopped reading and scanned the page. All this he already knew. He, like Runar, had seen a monster with his own eyes. He turned to the next page and started reading.

> . . . coat is covered with a special layer of dust, which is much more than the consequence of a messy way of life. The dust crystallizes the monster's nocturnal appearance, its ability to disappear into shadows and turn invisible in the right kind of twilight . . .

Koby repeated: "the monster's nocturnal appearance." What was that? Had they seen a glimpse of it in the forest the night before? When the monster suddenly froze and almost disappeared? Koby carried on reading.

> ... attempted to wash its left arm, or rather take the monster into the sauna to wash off the layer of dust. But the monster approached this operation with hostility and unwillingness, and therefore it was a failure. It was the only time I felt threatened in the monster's company. It reared up to its full height, raised its fists, and roared like a lion. Its eyes rolled like goldfish in a glass bowl ...

Goldfish in a glass bowl! Koby's eyes already sought the next heading: "Chapter 6: Observations of the Monster's Behavior."

There was such a lot of text. Koby was annoyed that he hadn't yet gotten round to learning the speed-reading technique. Reading the book would take ages. How would he know what was most important right now? It might be best to leaf through and read a bit from each page. Koby turned the page.

> ... expressionless face gives an impression of a dour nature. The monster seems withdrawn and unwilling. However, this is a mistaken interpretation. The more time I spent with the monster, the clearer it became that it is the gentlest and most peaceful humanoid animal, if not half-human ...

"Half-human," Koby repeated. The same word had been used in the letter Mom had received. Had someone else read this book too? And how had Runar come to the conclusion that the monster was half-human? This was the problem with reading bits here and there: you might have jumped over some important detail. He continued:

... half-human, which adapts quite well to human companionship. The monster's emotional states are conveyed not through its facial expressions, but, in my view, in its rolling eyes and the position of its shoulders. I think that by observing the monster's neck, shoulders, and eyes, one can keep up with its current feelings pretty accurately ...

Koby nodded, deep in thought. This information would no doubt be useful to them. He marked the page with a candy wrapper he found on the floor next to the beanbag chair. *Who's been eating candy in here?* he wondered in passing, and went on to the next spread.

... became attached to me to a notable degree during our weeks together. It showed its fondness not only by murring like a large cat, but also by doing me services it believed would please me. One day, to my surprise, it used its powerful arms to break a wooden bench into evenly sized firewood, which it stacked by the fireplace. It showed me its good deed, murring with happiness ...

Koby smiled to himself. Sounded like monsterish behavior. That morning, Grah had made them breakfast and piled so much cocoa powder in Halley's mug that the milk could no longer dissolve it to make it drinkable. The spoon had stood shuddering in the middle of the cocoa powder heap turned into paste. For Mimi, the monster had buttered eight slices of bread, which it then stacked into a wobbly tower.

But it was as clear as day that the monster had been taught human habits. Grah knew how to use the dishwasher and kettle. It knew that humans did not want monster dust in their food, and for the duration of breakfast had wrapped itself in a hooded apron, which almost totally prevented the monster dust from shedding. On its hands it had worn large, thin gloves, which allowed it to touch the food without everything turning gray.

In its protective clothing, Grah had looked like an astronaut. Koby had stared at its big, clumsy-looking hands, fascinated. How delicately the monster's fingers worked. Their dishes looked like dollhouse items in its hands, but the monster deftly picked up a little mug between two fingers and held it gently and carefully under the tap, turning on the faucet by nudging it with one finger. A single careless move would have broken both the mug and the tap. But Grah broke nothing. It did not make the slightest mistake. It was awesome.

After breakfast, Grah had tidied the kitchen, kind of.

Then it had withdrawn to its closet and closed the door. That was where it was now. Why? Had someone told it to get in the closet? It couldn't be particularly comfortable in there.

Koby moved on to the next chapter, which was titled "The Monster's Natural Environment."

> There is no doubt that monsters are outdoor creatures. Staying in human dwellings and living like humans is not only impossible for them, but probably also harmful.

Koby frowned. Harmful?

> It is true that it can be kept imprisoned in human structures for a time. In such cases, the most immediate problems are caused by the monster's dust layer, which quickly renders the cleanest environment into a filthy state. Naturally, problems may also be caused by the monster's unpleasant smell, which is at least partly caused by its diet, as well as its antagonistic approach to washing.
>
> The natural habitat for the monster is probably the forests of Finland. There are also some indications that the monster's abodes could be underground caves, soil pits, and other natural earthy shelters. I believe that the monster is a pack creature, even though it may sometimes move around on its own for long periods. However, in

the end it seeks out a monster pack to be with others of its kind. I also venture to argue that a human pack is not sufficient for a monster. It needs a larger, stronger, and wilder pack, or the color of its coat will start to fade and wither. I will return to this in more detail in "Chapter 12: Some Unusual Observations."

The monster is a creature that learns very easily. It learns to do humans' work in fields and in the home. However, this is not enough to make the monster happy. It is not a human but a free creature of nature.

At this point, we should also pay attention to the characteristic features of our own species, the humans. Would it be possible for us humans to live peaceful and mutually respectful lives alongside monsters? Or would we attempt to harness these gentle, strong beings as mere work animals to do our heaviest jobs? Regrettably often, human nature is far from humane, even though the misleading original meaning of the word is "human-like."

Koby's brow wrinkled. Was their situation precisely what Runar wrote about? Where had Grah come from? Where had it been before it came here? Did it even want to be in their home?

Despite all its animal qualities, the monster is very

human-like. It forms attachments, is emotional, and likes to communicate. It suffers just like a human if it is forced to live denying its own nature. And what is its nature? It is a free creature, independent of humans, not imprisoned in the crowded human world.

Koby stopped reading, shocked. Imprisoned in the crowded human world! At this very moment, Grah stood stuffed in the hall closet. Alone, without its pack. Forced here by humans. Not even a bit of freedom or forest, let alone a natural environment.

The door banged. Halley came in.

"Koby? Mimi?" Halley's excited voice called. "You'll never guess."

Koby put the book down and went into the hall, where Halley stood with three unfamiliar children. Koby nodded hi to them.

"What?" Mimi shouted from the bathroom.

"Is Mimi still in the bath?" Halley asked.

Koby shrugged.

"What will we never guess?" he asked.

"Oscar, Alice, and Minnie also have monsters," Halley replied triumphantly.

Koby nodded slowly and looked at the children, who stood in the monster-gray hall, looking tense.

"Did your moms and dads also go to Lapland?" Koby asked. Oscar and Minnie nodded.

"Did they win the trip in the lottery?" Koby went on. Oscar and Minnie nodded again.

"Very strange. They all won the grand prize," Koby said. Halley nodded. She had not thought of that.

"What are your monsters like?" Koby asked.

Oscar and Minnie exchanged looks.

"Ours is quite OK, I suppose," Oscar said lamely. "It smells really bad. But it doesn't hurt us or anything."

"My monster is really bad-tempered," Minnie complained. "It growls scarily if I don't eat the awful sandwiches it makes. It puts masses of cheese in them, and I loathe cheese, so I left and went to Oscar's, and I'm not going back. I'm not eating those sandwiches anymore."

Koby eyed the children thoughtfully. His monster expert's nose smelled trouble.

"Do your monsters know where you are now?" he asked.

"I don't think so," Oscar said.

"We sneaked out really quietly," Minnie explained.

"So where were the monsters?" Koby asked.

Halley chuckled. "You won't believe it, but Minnie's monster followed her to Oscar's. It stuffed itself into the same closet with Oscar and Alice's monster. Even though the closet's not really big enough for even one monster."

Oscar, Minnie, and Halley laughed, but Koby was thinking.

"Tell me," he said, "if the monster knew how to follow Minnie to Oscar's, why wouldn't it follow her here?"

Oscar, Minnie, and Halley stopped laughing and gaped at Koby. They hadn't thought of that, but now the thought filled their whole heads.

So it was hardly surprising that only Alice noticed an empty blue sleeve flash in the slightly opened bathroom door. It seemed to be beckoning her. She looked at the other children, who were staring at one another, worried. Nobody took any notice of Alice when she slipped into the bathroom unnoticed like a little blond shadow.

CHAPTER 10

Mimi in the Bath

INDEED, MIMI'S BATH HAD already taken a long time. The water had cooled, and Mimi's fingers had gone wrinkly ages ago. But still Mimi splashed around in the tub. She had had a long conversation with her bathrobe.

This is roughly how it had gone:

Mimi: This is getting really strange. I wish Mom were coming back soon.
Bathrobe: I see!
Mimi: But on the other hand, it was lucky Mom got to go to Lapland. Best lottery win ever.
Bathrobe: I wonder.
Mimi: Of course it is! We got the monster, too, and

Grah is so great. The paper that came with it said that . . .

Bathrobe: (jolly laughter)

Mimi: Why are you laughing?

Bathrobe: You humans! You believe everything you read. Even if you don't know who wrote it and why.

Mimi: Oh, so? What do you mean?

Bathrobe: Just think of me, little friend. My label says "100% cotton. Made in Portugal." And when I was bought, I was in a bag that said "Bathrobe. Cotton. Blue."

Mimi: Isn't it true, then?

Bathrobe: We-ell! True or not. I can tell you that I am 20% polyamide and only 80% cotton, and I was made in China. Does it matter? I don't know. Sometimes it does, sometimes not.

Mimi: What are you babbling on about? You're really weird today.

Bathrobe: No, I'm not. But weird things are happening in your home that may be dangerous.

Mimi: How do you mean? Is Grah dangerous?

Bathrobe: No. At least, not on purpose, but it is semi-wild, after all. But that isn't what I mean.

Mimi: What, then? Talk so that I can understand you.

Bathrobe: No, you have to think for yourself. Use your head.

Mimi: I'll throw you in the washing machine!

Bathrobe: Have you learned how to use the washing machine, my little friend? Don't splash that water everywhere! I am very absorbent. I'll give you three hints, if you want.

Mimi: Don't bother!

Bathrobe: I will anyway.

Mimi: Well, go on, then.

Bathrobe: The first hint is: There are other beings on the move, not just monsters.

Mimi: What else?

Bathrobe: Keep your eyes peeled. You, of everyone, notice unusual things. Here comes the second hint: I think it best if you all sleep elsewhere. Leave soon.

Mimi: Oh, why? And where else? In the yard?

Bathrobe: Decide for yourself. And here comes the third and final hint.

Just then the front door banged. Halley came home.

"Koby? Mimi?" Halley called. "You'll never guess!"

"What?" Mimi called from the bathroom.

The bathrobe froze but did not flop in a heap yet. Nobody answered Mimi.

"Well, they'll tell me soon," Mimi sniffed. "Yes, what were you saying?"

"Shhh!" hissed the bathrobe.

Mimi pricked up her ears but heard nothing.

"What's happening?" she whispered.

"Shhh!" the bathrobe hissed again.

They listened silently for a minute. How quiet a bathroom is when nobody is talking.

"Well, now," the bathrobe said then. "The situation has changed. You got a helper, a little girl called Alice. She's there in the hall. I'll get her in here right away."

"I don't know anybody called Alice," Mimi said.

"You will soon," the bathrobe said, and glided off the toilet straight to the door. There it gingerly peeked into the hall through the crack of the slightly opened door and then opened it a little more.

Mimi watched the bathrobe, amazed. It had never before tried to leave the bathroom. And it was not outside the bathroom now, but peeking into the hall. Anybody standing in the hall could see the bathrobe instantly, if they happened to look in the right direction at the right moment.

The bathrobe raised one of its empty sleeves and waved at someone in the hall. Then it nodded its hood, just to make sure. Then the bathrobe glided back to the toilet lid and sat down.

"Now we'll just wait, little friend," it said.

"What are we waiting for?" Mimi inquired.

"Just wait."

Suddenly the bathroom door opened a crack, and a small blond girl slipped inside. She stared at Mimi and the bathrobe with round, questioning eyes. The bathrobe gave a slight cough.

"Monster dust, excuse me," it apologized. "One can become pretty invisible under it, but it does irritate one's throat so."

"Hey," the girl said quietly. "I'm Alice."

"Well, now!" the bathrobe said, pleased. "Alice and Mimi. Get to know each other. Now I'm not needed anymore."

Empty and lifeless, it slid off the toilet lid and onto the floor.

"Oh," Alice gasped, startled.

"Bathrobe!" Mimi said. "What's the matter?"

But the bathrobe remained floppy and lifeless.

"I hope it's not dead," Mimi whispered, alarmed.

"It was so cool," Alice said.

"It *is* so cool," Mimi snapped.

"It asked me to come in here," Alice said. "I've never seen such a . . . bathrobe. I've just got an ordinary one. It can't walk or anything."

Mimi measured Alice with her eyes.

"The bathrobe said that you're my new helper. Something may be wrong, and we must sort it all out. And we may have to move out to the yard."

Alice nodded solemnly.

"That's what I thought," she replied. "That something isn't right."

Then Alice padded to the bathrobe lying in a heap on the floor, picked it up, and sat down on the toilet lid in the same spot where the bathrobe had sat a moment ago.

"Well, what do we do?" she asked.

CHAPTER 11

The Phone Call That Surprises Nobody

THE LANDLINE PHONE IN the hall rang. Halley and Koby looked at each other. The only one to call that phone was Invisible Voice, who should be turning up at home in a couple of hours. Something was amiss.

"Halley, take Oscar and Minnie into our room," Koby said. "Wait there. This won't take long."

Halley nodded. She understood what Koby was thinking. An invisible dad was too strange a thing to explain to Oscar and Minnie. At least so soon.

"What are we waiting for?" Oscar wondered aloud.

The phone rang again.

"Where's your monster?" Minnie asked hesitantly.

"In that closet right behind you. Go on," Koby said, hurrying them. Minnie jumped and promptly headed toward the children's bedroom. Oscar followed her. The phone rang again.

"Why doesn't anybody pick up? It must be Invisible Voice—answer it!" Mimi called from the bathroom.

Koby cleared his throat and picked up the receiver.

"Koby Hellman," he said. "Oh, Dad. Where are you?"

Mimi appeared at the bathroom door in her blue bathrobe. Alice peeked over her shoulder.

"Told you. It's Invisible Voice," Mimi confirmed to Alice.

"What's that?" Alice queried.

"Nothing," Halley answered, and almost pushed Minnie and Oscar into their bedroom. "Wait here," she said, closing the door.

"I need to talk to Invisible Voice—give me the phone," Mimi urged, holding her hand out. Koby dodged her and went on talking.

"It's Mimi, yes. She wants to talk to you in a minute," Koby said, then made a face at Mimi and turned his back.

"Fine, fine. Of course we've eaten. Mimi just came out of her bath. It's not strange—Mimi often takes a bath during the day. Yes, well. Oh, what? The blizzard continues? Still? And the whole airport is closed. Oh dear. Really bad."

Koby listened silently for a while, nodding.

"It can't be helped. The monster makes really great food. It even knows how to use the dishwasher. Yes. Yeah,

Mom's having a nice time in Lapland. Call us again when you know when the airport will open again. Yes, we'll let Mom know.

"I'll give the phone to Mimi now," Koby finally said. Then he covered the receiver with his hand and whispered to Mimi: "Not a word about other monsters or last night or the monster book or anything, understand?"

"Yeah, yeah," Mimi muttered, and took the receiver.

"Hello, is this Invisible Voice?" she said, and then nodded, pleased. "So you're not coming, then? I heard! I've got ears. I wanted to tell you that it's very strange here. The bathrobe just said that we had better go out to the yard soon and stay there. Do you see, a bit like an escape."

Mimi listened a moment.

"No, it's true," she giggled. "It's not a silly story. The bathrobe said that a girl called Alice is my helper from now on, and that there are other creatures here apart from monsters. We must use our heads now, to cope. But the bathrobe says that if anybody can use their head, I can. That's why everything is actually my responsibility from now on."

Mimi listened for a moment before continuing her babbling: "Alice is my helper. But listen now. As soon as the bathrobe said that, it went all floppy and didn't say anything else. What do you think: can a bathrobe die?"

Mimi listened again and frowned, insulted.

"Alice is no imaginary friend. Alice is right here and

can come to the phone this minute. And about monsters, you can—"

Koby snatched the phone from Mimi's hand and shook his head furiously. Mimi sighed and padded off toward their bedroom, followed by Alice. Koby sighed and put the receiver to his own ear.

"Hullo, Koby here again. Yes, yes. The bathrobe and Alice and the monster. It's probably quite normal, just a phase. It's not a problem. Do you want to talk to Halley? She can tell you—" Koby began, but Halley, standing in front of their bedroom door, shook her head hard.

"Oh, Halley's just gone to the bathroom and can't talk," Koby said, and Halley nodded.

"Of course, Dad," Koby assured the phone. "We'll take care of each other. We're quite all right as long as I'm here."

Halley huffed disdainfully.

"Bye-bye," said Koby, and put the phone down. He looked at Halley. Halley looked at him.

"Invisible Voice isn't coming today, either?" Halley confirmed.

"No, he's not. The airport is closed because of the blizzard, and they don't know when it will reopen," Koby replied.

Halley wasn't sure if this was bad or good news. Of course, it's good if children have an adult at home. But sometimes, in certain situations, it's good if the children have a little time to figure out the strange things that have crossed their path. Right now the Hellman children had such a situation.

"I think we need to plan what to do now," Koby said. "Let's go to our room."

Halley nodded in agreement.

CHAPTER 12

Another Strange Creature

I T WAS DARK IN the children's bedroom. The blinds were tightly shut and the lights off. Oscar, Minnie, Mimi, and Alice sat in a circle on the floor turning their heads this way and that, as if looking for something.

"Why are you sitting in the dark?" Koby asked.

"Let's turn on the light," Halley said.

"No!" called Mimi. "Something is flying around in here. We're trying to see it."

"You see better with the light on," said Halley.

"No!" Mimi called again. "It's got a light itself."

"Yes, it has," Minnie confirmed. "Like a firefly, but bigger. I almost saw it."

"Almost, right," Koby echoed, looking around. "Can't see anything now."

"I almost saw it too," Oscar said. "It was like a frog or something."

"A flying frog with a light," Koby mused aloud, and looked at the ceiling. There was no sign anywhere of anything that was at all like a flying frog.

"Yes," Mimi said. "What's more, the bathrobe said that there are others on the move, apart from monsters. Best keep our eyes peeled."

"Please, no more about that bathrobe," Halley asked.

"I saw the bathrobe too," Alice said excitedly. "It was cool!"

"What did you see?" Minnie asked, puzzled.

"Nothing," Halley grumbled.

"The bathrobe. But now it's dead," Mimi went on glumly.

Halley suppressed a laugh.

"You mustn't laugh," Alice said with disapproval. "It may really have died."

"What are you talking about—what bathrobe has died?" Oscar asked.

"Mimi's imaginary friend. Or former friend. Since it's dead now," Halley said. "Pity it didn't have time to say anything else before it died."

"It did," Mimi snapped, hurt. "It said that we had better leave here as soon as possible. Move out to the yard. And that if anybody can, I can work it all out, because I have the most wits about me."

Halley glanced at Koby and grinned. Koby grinned back but felt a little unsure. He knew that the bathrobe could at least sit up and move its sleeves.

"There!" Minnie yelled suddenly. "There, above the bookcase."

"I saw it too!" Halley shrieked, excited. "Or at least some kind of a light, but where did it go?"

"Where?" Koby asked. He was annoyed that he was never as quick as Halley.

"I didn't see it," Alice whispered, frightened.

"Let's be really quiet," Minnie suggested. "Perhaps it'll show itself again."

Six pairs of eyes peered around the room, from the ceiling to the floor, everywhere. They saw nothing special.

All of a sudden, Minnie sprang up, startled.

"What is it?" Halley whispered.

"S-something d-dropped on me," Minnie stammered.

"Turn on the light," Koby ordered.

The light clicked on, and the children rushed to surround Minnie.

"Are you OK?" Halley asked, worried.

"Can't see anything," Koby said, frowning. "What was it that dropped on you?"

"Who threw candy wrappers on the floor?" Mimi asked. "Trash should be put in the trash can, not on our bedroom floor! In any case, we have a rule that candy must be offered to everybody."

The others eyed Mimi, puzzled.

"We have no candy," Oscar said.

"So where did those come from?" Mimi pointed at the floor next to Minnie.

Indeed, on the floor was a pile of shiny candy wrappers. Oscar picked up one crumpled paper and unrolled it.

"From some place abroad," he said. "Strange letters, can't read it."

Koby studied another one. "I've never seen such letters," he said.

"Perhaps it's that flying frog's candy," Alice said in a little voice.

Instantly Koby remembered where he had seen an identical wrapper before: this morning, when he had been reading the monster book. He had picked up a candy wrapper just like this off the floor to use as a bookmark.

"Alice could be right," Koby said. "These candy wrappers don't belong to any of us. The monster doesn't eat candy. Perhaps the bathrobe was right and there are others here, apart from us."

"Koby, please!" Halley exclaimed, but Koby continued:

"Let's turn the light back off. We'll wait. It'll show itself."

They turned out the light and sat back down on the floor to wait.

"Another candy wrapper dropped," Minnie whispered, but not scared anymore.

"Perhaps it can fly in the dark, too," Oscar suggested.

"Another one down," Minnie whispered.

"Why are they only dropping on Minnie?" Halley asked.

"Good question," Oscar said.

Koby raised his eyes to just above Minnie. In the semi-darkness, they could just make out the plastic bedroom light shaped like a Peter Pan ship.

"What if it's Peter Pan?" Mimi whispered, enchanted.

"Peter Pan doesn't look like a frog," Halley said, smiling in the dark. "Or eat candy. Or exist."

"How do you know?" Mimi asked. "Monsters didn't used to exist either."

Koby got up and crept to the light switch by the door.

"All of you, look at the ship. Now," he whispered.

He clicked the light on. The pale blue plastic ship swayed slightly below the ceiling. There was not a single frog or Peter Pan in sight.

"I'll get the step stool from the kitchen," Koby said. "Keep an eye on the lamp."

A moment later, Koby was back with the kitchen stool. He positioned it below the lamp and carefully climbed up.

"What do you see?" Oscar asked tensely.

"Is it Peter Pan?" Alice asked quietly. She was afraid

of Peter Pan. She had always been afraid that one evening Peter Pan would knock on her window. That was why Alice never slept with the window open, not even on the hottest summer nights.

"Wow," Koby whispered, and stared into the ship-shaped ceiling light. "It's not Peter Pan or a frog. It's—"

"What?" Halley asked, agitated.

"I don't know," Koby said. "Perhaps it's some kind of a flying troll. Or a fairy. It has wings and . . ."

"A fairy!" Mimi repeated, delighted. "I want to see the fairy!"

"There's loads of that candy in here," Koby said. "Whatever it is seems to be afraid of the light. It's holding its hands over its eyes, so I can't see its face."

"Bring it down," Mimi asked.

"Hey, creature," Koby whispered kindly. "Do you understand me? Can I get you out of there?"

"Ee, ee, ee." The creature made squeaky noises. *"Oo, oo, oo."*

Koby gently put his hand out. "Come here." He spoke as if to a frightened kitten.

Suddenly the doorbell rang, demanding and loud. *Ding dong!* Everyone jumped, including the fairy in the ceiling lamp.

"It's frightened—now it's flying off!" Koby called.

The flying fairy-troll shot out of the ceiling lamp. Candy papers and candy rattled down to the floor. Now everybody saw the creature clearly. At least, as clearly as it is possible to see a creature that flies fast, zigzagging around the room.

"Oh!" Minnie yelled. "A flying troll!"

"A sparkling troll." Mimi sighed. "Look at its tiny hands. What is it carrying?"

"Candy wrappers, of course," Minnie replied.

The doorbell rang again, but nobody wanted to answer it now.

"Where did it fly?" Koby asked, turning his head fast from side to side.

"It vanished," Mimi said. "Shall we turn out the light again?"

Whoever was ringing the bell was clearly getting irate. It rang again, more furiously: *ding dong, ding dong, ding dong, ding dong!*

"Who's the crazy person at the door?" Halley shouted, and covered her ears. "You don't ring the doorbell like that!"

The ringing was now constant.

"Can someone answer the door!" Mimi called, holding her ears. "Quick! Hurts my ears!"

"Look through the peephole to see who it is!" Koby yelled.

Oscar and Halley ran into the hall. Halley pushed a stool to the door and climbed up to look through the peephole.

"Two monsters," Halley said, taken aback.

Oscar climbed up next to Halley and looked through the peephole.

Indeed, behind the door stood two huge black-gray monsters. They were similar to Grah yet looked quite different. One of them in particular looked scary and cross, and it was its fat finger that was pressed on the doorbell: *ding dong ding dong ding dong ding dong ding dong . . .*

"Open it, quick!" Koby shouted from the bedroom door.

"Those are our monsters. Minnie's monster is ringing

the bell!" Oscar shouted to Koby over the din, and then looked at Halley, frightened. "How did they find us?"

"What did I tell you," Koby muttered.

Halley looked at Koby, as if asking him what to do. The doorbell donging was ringing in her ears, and it wasn't easy to think clearly.

"Open it! They're not going anywhere. We have no choice but to open the door!" Koby yelled.

CHAPTER 13

The Fairy-Frog Attacks

Halley, Koby, Oscar, and Minnie sat on the rustling trash bags covering the couch, browsing the contacts on their phones. Oscar had a notebook on his knees, in which he had written down some names.

"Who else?" Halley asked.

"Jemima?" Koby suggested. "Check, please, Oscar."

Oscar ran his finger down the list of names.

"Sent already," he said.

"Sophie?" Koby continued.

"Sent," Oscar said.

"What about Maya and Jack?" Halley proposed.

"The names aren't on the list," Oscar confirmed.

"Let's send it off, then," said Halley. "Copy message— Just a minute—this is going to Maya's number."

Hi! If you, too, have a M
in the closet (we have),
come to the edge of the
forest near the marina,
by the soccer field
goals, today at nine p.m.
Check your floors for
foreign candy wrappers
or if anything lit-up is
flying around. We'll talk
more then. Best wishes,
Halley, Koby, Oscar, and
Minnie

"There, the twentieth message," Halley said, pleased. "What time is it?"

"Almost four," Koby said. "They'll come out soon to cook dinner."

Koby turned to look toward the hall.

All three monsters had squashed themselves into the hall closet. First they had squeezed into the Hellmans' hall, then the closet. It was too small even for one monster. For three monsters, it was quite definitely too tight. Three monsters simply could not fit in there. But it seemed to satisfy the monsters that even a part of their bodies fit inside the closet.

Grah was completely in the closet, squashed flat

against the back wall like a hairy caterpillar. Perhaps it was Grah's privilege, as it was its closet. Oscar and Alice's monster had stuffed its right side, right leg, right arm, and whole head, which rested on Grah's shoulder, into the closet. Minnie's monster had squeezed the left side of its body in. Its head rested on Grah's other shoulder.

The new monsters had pretty fat bellies, and their stomachs were tightly pressed together. It actually looked as if they had gotten stuck in the doorway by their bellies. In spite of everything, the monsters looked peaceful and happy. All had their eyes closed and were breathing evenly.

"They're unlikely to be asleep," Koby had explained to Oscar and Minnie. "Could be that they've just been trained to go in the closet to wait, whenever they're not taking care of the housework or us."

Then Koby told Minnie and Oscar a few important facts from Runar's book. Mimi told them once more what the bathrobe had told her. Oscar and Minnie described how the monsters had come to their homes (in the same way as to the Hellmans'), how their parents had left, just like their mom, winning a trip to Lapland in a lottery.

"Every ticket was a winner," Halley said.

"But why?" Koby wondered aloud. "Why would someone send our parents on vacation in Lapland and send monsters as nannies?"

"It did say in the letter that this is an experiment," Halley said.

"A monster experiment," Oscar said.

"And a human experiment at the same time," Koby added.

"Perhaps we should also do a few experiments," Halley said.

And that was how they came to be sitting on the rustling sofa, sending text messages to all the people they knew. Because the first matter to be investigated was this: Were there more monsters than these three?

They had concluded that if there were more monsters, it was best to gather someplace with more room. The Hellman apartment couldn't take any more monsters. And they didn't need to invite the monsters personally, as they followed the children in their charge.

Koby and Halley had drafted the message. It had been tricky. The message had to be at the same time mysterious (in case the recipient knew nothing about monsters) and easily understood (in case the recipient was not very quick-witted).

"Wonder what Mimi and Alice are up to?" Koby asked, eyes toward their bedroom.

"I'm sure they're OK," Halley said coolly.

"At least they have the lights on now," Koby went on.

Mimi and Alice had been upset that their names had been left out of the text message. Halley had wanted to save characters. She didn't want the message to be too long; there were so many names already. And Mimi and Alice were little kids nobody even knew! Children their age didn't have their own phones. It made sense that their names should be left off the message.

So Mimi and Alice had stormed out of the living room and gone into the bedroom, slamming the door. After sitting there for a while, Mimi decided that they could show up the bigger kids by trapping the flying creature.

The girls had turned out the light and were sitting in the dim room. When Koby came to the door to make peace, Mimi yelled: "Go away! We're studying the flying troll!"

Of course, Koby had gone away. He had better things to do than worry about his little sister.

Halley's phone bleeped.

"Here we go!" Minnie exclaimed. "Who's sending the first reply?"

Halley stared at her phone screen, frowning.

> What M? Have you gone
> mad, Halley? I don't
> know anyone called
> Oscar. Bye, Erica

"Erica doesn't have a monster," Halley said.

"I got a message too!" Oscar said.

"And I think I got a second—no, third one," Halley said.

Messages arrived, the phones bleeping like a chorus of baby birds.

"Let's read them aloud," Koby ordered. "Oscar, write the answers on the list."

Oscar nodded. Halley, Koby, and Minnie started reading the messages.

Minka: This text was sent to the wrong number? Wanna go swimming tomorrow?

Jemima: We have a M. I'll be there.

Aron: Yeah we do.

Joel: Whaat???????

Olly: Er, too many detective books? I don't get it . . .

Alba: Yeah. Me and
Jenna are coming.

Leo: Yep. I have a M.

The children's bedroom door opened abruptly. Mimi stood at the door in her blue bathrobe, smiling triumphantly. Alice was grinning behind her. Mimi was holding a brown paper bag that was moving. It looked as if there were a battery-operated rubber ball inside it.

"What's that?" Halley asked.

"Wouldn't you like to know," Mimi answered, and patted the bag gently.

"That's why I asked, dumbhead," Halley muttered, rolling her eyes.

"Did you catch the flying troll?" Koby asked with interest.

Mimi and Alice glanced at each other.

"We did!" Alice yelled, and couldn't hold back a gleeful giggle any longer. "We caught the fairy-troll, and it's in this bag."

The others quickly jumped to their feet.

"Show us," Halley said, but Mimi snatched the bag away.

"Stop," she said importantly. "One thing you should know. It has a weapon."

"A weapon?" Koby repeated.

"Really?" Oscar asked, concerned.

"Yes. A kind of spike," Alice explained.

"A sharp spike," Mimi said emphatically.

"You mean a bit like a needle?" Minnie asked.

"Maybe," Mimi answered, nodding.

"We didn't get a good look at it," Alice explained.

"If it has a sharp spike, why doesn't it escape from that bag? The bag is paper," Koby asked.

Did the creature bouncing around in the bag understand human speech? Or was it a mere coincidence that as soon as Koby spoke, the first ripping sound was heard? A small, sharp spike pierced the paper bag and began to tear a hole in it, persistently twisting and stabbing.

"It's poking through the bag! It's going to get away!" Mimi shouted. Alice began to scream and jump up and down.

"Let's get out of here!" Oscar yelled, and hid behind Halley's back.

"Quick, get something hard, like a bucket!" Halley called, but nobody moved an inch. Nobody fetched the bucket, because, as if bewitched, they were all staring at the hole, which was getting bigger and bigger every moment. The needle-like spike was sharp and the user extremely quick.

In a few seconds, the tear was big enough, and out peeked a tiny, snub-nosed, and greenish face, undeniably a little like a frog or a bulldog. Two bright water-colored eyes flitted belligerently every which way, staring at the children. A thin brownish-green hand appeared in the tear and wagged the spike menacingly.

"Now it'll attack," Alice piped up, terrified.

"No . . . what's up with it now?" Halley asked.

The creature had frozen on the spot. Its minute nostrils fluttered. It turned its head, slow and majestic, like a bloodhound. It was no longer interested in the children. It had noticed something else.

A low growling sound was coming from the hall closet, like a giant cat purring.

"I don't believe it," Halley whispered.

The monsters had woken up. Their wild yellow eyes were open and looking straight at the spiky creature peeking from the bag, who was staring back at the monsters.

"Perhaps they know each other," Mimi whispered to Alice.

There was a popping sound when the monsters, wedged in the doorway by their bellies, yanked themselves loose. Growling menacingly, the monsters turned toward the creature. They no longer appeared clumsy and heavy. Every movement was smooth and controlled. All of a sudden, the monsters were magnificent, strong, and very dangerous. Their yellow gazes were fixed on the creature waving its spike.

Peering out from the bag, the fairy-troll let out a defiant

shriek. It shook its silvery spike fiercely and squawked: *"Ah-ah-ah!"*

Then it slashed the paper bag with its little sword so that the tear was twice as big.

The creature shot out of the bag, spike at the ready, squealing: *"Ah-ah-ah! Ee-ee-ee!"* It flew in a wild circle in the air.

The monsters' growling became louder. It was beginning to sound very threatening.

"Can we get out of here?" Minnie asked in a tiny voice, and sidled behind Halley, where Oscar was already cowering.

"Ah-ah-ah-ah!" squealed the flying frog creature, darting about.

"Let's go," Koby said nervously.

"Where to?" Mimi asked, looking in turns at the flying fairy buzzing on one side of them and the growling monsters on the other. They were in the middle of an imminent fight, and with no escape route. Alice let out a sob and grabbed Mimi's hand. Mimi squeezed tight to comfort her and slipped her other hand into her bathrobe pocket. It was almost like holding the bathrobe's hand.

Now the flying frog made a ferocious dive and shot straight toward the monsters. It was attacking.

"Watch out!" Halley managed to call before there was a cloud of dust, and everything disappeared in an all-pervading gray-black cloud.

CHAPTER 14

Koby Has an Idea

T HE STAIRWELL WAS SILENT and echoey, but at least there wasn't one speck of monster dust floating around. The children went down the stairs, coughing. Koby held Mimi tightly by the hand. Mimi held Alice's hand; she was coughing and spluttering. Alice's other hand was held by Oscar, who with his other hand pulled Minnie, her eyes so full of monster dust that she couldn't see anything.

"Three more steps," Oscar said to Minnie, who was gingerly feeling her way, her eyes squeezed shut. "Left turn now, then a few steps. Here's a threshold, don't trip, good . . . Now we're in the bike storage room."

Alice coughed and coughed. Koby led the chain of children through the bike room toward another door.

"There's a sink; Minnie can wash her eyes, and Alice can have a drink of water," Koby said.

What had happened back in their apartment on the fifth floor was amazing and terrible at the same time. The monsters had let off some kind of a dust bomb. All the dust, black smoke, or whatever it was had puffed out of the monsters' matted, ragged coats—as if beneath the thick fur there were hidden a thousand dust capsules waiting to be discharged. And then: *PUFFF!* Showers of dust!

It was probably a monster defense mechanism, Koby thought. Like a skunk's stink shower. Perhaps Runar knew something about this. They had to get the book from upstairs as soon as possible. But not yet. Not until the dust had settled. Not until the attack upstairs was definitely over. Koby still shuddered at the memory of the monsters' whirring hum and the flying fairy attack.

"There's the sink," Koby said, clicking on the light in the basement corridor. "You can wash your faces here. I'll get an old towel from our basement storage. Oscar, can you give Alice a drink?"

Koby left the others coughing by the sink and went off. He wanted to be alone for a minute. It was exhausting to not understand what was happening around you.

Koby pushed the key into the lock on the thick metal door and turned it. The heavy security door opened unexpectedly easily and almost silently. Koby stepped into the narrow passage between the wire storage cages. In the basement everything was just as it always was. It was comforting. The storage cages overflowed with stuff: balcony furniture, battered suitcases, skis and sleds, high chairs, old newspapers, rolled-up rugs.

Koby walked to the end of the passage and stopped by the last storage cage. It was their cage, and it was overflowing with nothing. Mom had left it tidy and organized. There were handy storage shelves on the walls, and on the shelves were boxes upon which Mom had neatly written the contents: WINTER CLOTHES (KIDS), OLD DISHES SET, CAMPING GEAR + CAMP STOVE, TENT, SLEEPING BAGS . . .

Camping gear and sleeping bags, Koby thought while opening the cage door. Why did they have camping gear, when nobody ever went camping? The idea of the family camping almost made him laugh.

But suddenly Koby realized that he had walked straight into the solution. The whole apartment was full of choking gray dust and . . . whatever. The bathrobe had been right: they could not stay there. But where would they go? Grandma's house was far away, and they had no vacation cabin. The solution was camping, of course! And for camping, you needed camping gear, tents, and sleeping bags. Camp stove, absolutely!

Koby climbed onto the step stool that was kept in the basement storage. He reached up and grabbed the camping gear box, but it was too heavy to get down. He needed Halley to help.

Koby jumped off the stool and ran the whole length of the passage back to the sink. The others now looked almost clean. Most of the dust had been washed off, and Alice had stopped coughing.

"Have you got the towel?" Oscar put his hand out, dripping with gray water.

"Oh, no, sorry, I forgot," Koby answered, out of breath. "Where's Halley?"

A silence descended on the basement corridor; the only sound was the calming hiss of the tap they had left running. Indeed, where was Halley? Had she walked down the stairs with them? Had anyone held her hand? Had anyone seen Halley in the basement? An ominous thought descended like a storm cloud.

"Halley got left behind upstairs." Mimi's voice was shrill. "Come, Alice, let's go."

"Stop!" Koby shouted. "Not yet! Let's think!"

But all that was left of Mimi and Alice was the slam of the door. The girls had gone.

CHAPTER 15

Halley's Observations

So, where was Halley? At home, of course, on the fifth floor. She sat in the kitchen, covered from head to foot in gray dust, with a piece of paper towel in front of her mouth serving as a mask. Monster dust made you cough.

On the floor lay a toy fishing net, bought on the beach the previous summer. It was in shreds. In the middle of the kitchen table stood a glass cookie jar, inside which a tiny, angry creature with a spike dashed about, jabbing at the jar walls with its weapon.

The creature was so odd-looking that one would have thought Halley was sitting there staring at it. But no. Halley was craning her neck to see into the hall, squinting.

The mail slot opened.

"Halley, are you in there?" Mimi whispered. "We came to rescue you. Give us a sign if you can hear this."

"Could you open the door for Mimi?" Halley asked Oscar's monster, who was standing nearest to the door. The monster, looking sad and defeated, turned obediently to the door.

Mimi and Alice slipped into the hall and bumped into the monster.

"Uh-oh, oops!" Mimi exclaimed, backing off quickly. She looked around. "Halley? Where are you?"

"Here, in the kitchen," Halley replied.

The monster slouched back to the wall, a dust-gray cloth hanging from its hand. It had been washing the wall. Minnie's monster stood in front of the gray-streaked bathroom door, wiping it down. The rug was gone, perhaps taken to the balcony.

"So they're cleaning up now?" Mimi asked, surprised. Halley nodded.

"Of course. Whoever makes a mess cleans it up. That's the rule we have."

"Where's Grah?" Mimi asked.

"Cleaning the living room," Halley said. "That's not as dirty as in here. But Grah is so embarrassed that it may start crying again. I hope it doesn't. If it could talk, it would probably be saying sorry all the time. That dust bomb was something they're really not supposed to do. I said to the monsters, 'No worries, we'll clean up now.'

And they immediately started cleaning. Where are all the others?"

"In the basement. We thought that you were in mortal danger," Mimi said. "But you seem to be quite all right, and you even got that fairy into a jar!"

"Come and see," Halley said, nodding proudly. "It was quite easy to catch, but it managed to tear the net to shreds. Look at that spike. It's not a sword."

"What is it, then?" Mimi asked, staring at the angry creature darting here and there. "I can't see — it moves too fast."

"It'll tire itself out soon," Halley said. "Then look at the spike really closely."

Mimi put her face up to the cookie jar. The creature stopped and hovered on the spot, wings buzzing, staring defiantly at her.

"It's got a lovely little nose and funny sticky-out ears! And its skin is just like a frog's," Mimi said.

"Check out the spike now, before it's on the move again," Halley told her.

Mimi looked. The spike was metallic, hollow, and quite pointy. The creature held it tightly in one hand. The upper part of the spike was as sharp as a newly sharpened pencil, but only on one side.

"Looks a bit like a drinking straw," Mimi said. "One of those straws you use to poke a hole in a juice box."

"Exactly," Halley said. Mimi was really quite clever for a little sister.

"Is it a straw? What does it drink through it?" Alice wondered. "Shall we give it some juice? See if it can drink?"

"Where did you leave all the others?" Halley asked. "Can you go get them? Koby will want to see this, I'm sure."

"Are you OK staying here alone with all these monsters?" Mimi asked.

"What do you think?" Halley said. "Go on. Fetch Koby, quickly."

"OK, we're going. We'll be real quick. Don't be scared," Mimi said. "Come on, Alice!"

About five minutes later, the front door lock rattled again. Someone was turning a key in the lock. The door opened slowly, as if hesitating. To open or not?

"Who is it?" Halley called out.

"There's nothing dangerous in here," came a loud voice from behind the door. "Just open the door, you dumbheads! Halley's in the kitchen, and the monsters are all cleaning up with their aprons on!"

"Mimi, is that you?" Halley called out. "Is Koby there?"

The door opened wide.

"Come inside, cowards, there's nothing to be scared of," Halley said.

Koby, Oscar, and Minnie stepped cautiously into the hall. Mimi and Alice tried to push past them, but they seemed to think that Mimi and Alice needed protection.

"Argh, let me go!" Mimi snapped, but Koby kept her tightly behind him.

"Let's check the latch," he said.

"Quite safe," Halley said. "Did Mimi tell you that the flying creature's spike is really a straw?"

"I told him!" Mimi yelled crossly from behind Koby.

"Come and see for yourselves," Halley said. "And stop being such chickens! There's nothing to be afraid of!"

"It really is a straw," Koby said, his face flat against the cookie jar.

"What does it use it for? Surely not for drinking."

"For drinking, specifically," Halley said. "I happened to see."

"Did it drink juice?" Alice murmured.

"Not juice," Halley said, looking at each of them in turn. It was good to be the one with the most information, for once. Was this how Koby felt all the time?

"Well, tell us," Oscar said, rushing her.

"You may have noticed that the monsters really didn't like that creature," Halley began.

"Yes?" the others asked in chorus.

"Well, I know why. You see, as soon as you had scampered off and run away—"

"We did not run away!" Mimi shouted, insulted.

"Well, where did you run to, then?" Halley asked kindly.

"Oh, whatever, just tell us," Koby urged, frowning at Mimi.

Halley smiled smugly and went on: "So, as soon as the rest of you ran out of here like little bunny rabbits, that straw fairy attacked. It dashed straight into the dust cloud the monsters had let off, screaming horribly, and attacked the nearest monster. It happened to be Minnie's fat-bellied monster, the angry one."

"Oh!" Minnie exclaimed.

"What did it do to the monsters?" Koby asked.

"At first I couldn't see properly, there was so much dust. But as soon as the monsters began to move, the dust cloud dispersed a little. Of course I thought that the spike was a sword and the flying troll was going to poke it at the monsters."

"But it's not a sword!" Mimi shouted, triumphant.

"Listen! The flying troll flew straight at Minnie's monster, stabbed the straw into its arm, and started to suck its blood through the straw. Just like a big juice box! It's not a fairy but a monster mosquito that sucks their blood. Or whatever it is that flows in the monsters' veins."

"That's horrid," said Mimi with disgust, looking at the fairy in the cookie jar. "A nasty, whining mosquito. I thought it was a fairy."

"It might still be a fairy," Halley said. "What do we know about fairies? Perhaps they are blood-suckers."

"Could it attack a human?" Oscar asked, worried. "What if—"

"Halley, what happened then?" Koby interrupted. "What did the monster do?"

"It was really scared. It froze on the spot and whined.

Same with the other monsters: they froze like snowmen. And all the time that horrible little mosquito thing was sucking the blood out of Minnie's monster."

"Ick!" Mimi said disapprovingly, and wrinkled her nose.

"What happened then?" Koby asked.

"When it had drunk a bellyful, it pulled the straw out. But it must have had too much, because it couldn't fly properly anymore. Its wings couldn't carry it, so it drifted slowly to the floor like some autumn leaf and flopped on its back. I got the net from the balcony and caught it," Halley continued.

"What happened to the monster?" Minnie asked, concerned. After all, it was her monster.

"Well, the same thing that happens when a mosquito sucks your blood. Nothing. See for yourself."

The children checked out Minnie's monster, who was scrubbing the bathroom door frame.

"Looks normal," Mimi said.

"So it does," Minnie confirmed.

"We should examine the sting site," Koby said thoughtfully.

"What do we do now?" Oscar asked, worried.

"The fairy is in the jar, and the monsters are cleaning," Halley answered. "What more should we do, do you suppose?"

"I'm going to wash my bathrobe," Mimi said, studying her sleeves. The blue waffle cloth had disappeared under gray, fluffy dust.

Alice tittered and immediately sneezed.

"We need to go to the supermarket," Halley said. "Koby, shall we go?"

"We?" Koby asked, surprised. The two of them had never done the shopping before. In any case, there was plenty of food in the cupboard; after all, Mom had only left the day before.

"Yes, *we*," Halley said, staring at Koby in an odd way.

"What's wrong with you?" Koby asked. "We don't need to go shopping."

"Yes, we do," Halley said, then whispered to Koby very quietly: "We need to talk."

Koby frowned.

"What are you whispering about?" Oscar asked.

"I'm not whispering," Halley snapped.

"You were," Koby said. "But I couldn't make out what you said. I don't think there's any point in going shopping."

"Argh," Halley grunted at Koby. "Whatever. If you don't get it, you don't get it. Let everybody hear it, then. I have a feeling that the monsters can turn invisible with the help of that dust."

"Well, I can see them quite easily," Mimi said, before

disappearing with giggling Alice into the bathroom to figure out how to get the washing machine to work. Surely it couldn't be that hard?

Halley went on, looking at Koby: "After you had run off and the monsters had started cleaning, I sat at the kitchen table and watched. When there's a lot of dust, it's just dust, a bit like a shadow. But when it settles, you don't see it anymore. Then it starts to work."

"What do you mean, 'work'?" Oscar asked.

Halley went on: "Well, suddenly the monsters simply vanished from view. I saw them in the hall, and then I saw nothing in the hall. I thought they had run away or gone into another room. But as soon as they moved, I could see them again. I think that if they stand quite still in their own dust, they can be invisible."

"How could that be possible?" Koby mumbled to himself.

In the bathroom, the washing machine started. Mimi and Alice had figured it out.

CHAPTER 16

Guarding the Door

HALLEY SAT WITH HER back against the front door and tried to stay awake. She was on door watch, and naturally you couldn't sleep on watch. Halley's job was to keep the monsters in the hall while Oscar and Minnie went to look for camping gear. Because tonight they would all move out to the yard.

How would Halley stop the monsters from going after their charges, if they really decided to go? Anyone else might have thought about it, perhaps even worried. But Halley did not bother her head with the matter. She would think of something. For now there were other things to think of. Like what to tell the absent parents.

Invisible Voice had phoned again. The blizzard was still going on. The passengers had been told that the airport would be closed at least another twenty-four hours.

Invisible Voice had been worried and said that they must phone Mom in Lapland. Koby had told him that they couldn't call Mom, but they could send her a text message.

Just an hour earlier Mom had sent them the message:

Is Dad at home now?

Halley sighed. You had to be really careful with words. You couldn't tell outright lies, but you had to stretch the facts a bit. But not so stretched that Mom became suspicious.

Of course, they couldn't tell Mom that Invisible Voice was stuck in a snowdrift. Otherwise she would come straight back, and that would help nobody. So they had told her:

Hi, Mom! All good, as
before. Just washed the
walls with the monster.
Dad sends love and says
home is the best place
in the world. We have
friends over and may go
for sleepover or picnic.
Bye-bye. Love from: all
at home

All of that was true in a way. Invisible Voice had sent his love on the phone. He had said that home was the best place in the world. Although such a phrase from Invisible Voice was so strange in Halley's view that Mom was bound to suspect something. But Koby would not agree to lie anymore.

Mom had replied right away:

> Good! Don't overdo the
> cleaning. No need to
> wash the walls. All's well
> here, if a little boring.
> We have no planned
> activities. The camp is
> unusual in many ways.
> Tomorrow we'll go to a
> spa. They told us that
> we can all sleep today or
> go for a hike. I, for one,
> am not sleepy! Off for a
> hike, then.

Halley yawned. If only she could sleep! She had slept far too little last night. She scanned the hall walls, just to keep awake. The monsters had spent ages scrubbing them. Then they had stayed around the kitchen door, restless. The mosquito-fairy made them nervous.

"We'll have to hide that spike creature so that the monsters can settle down," Koby had said.

So Halley and Oscar had tapped a few air holes in the cookie jar lid using a nail and hammer, so that the fairy, or whatever it was, wouldn't suffocate. Then they had shoved the jar in a top cupboard in the kitchen.

"It's your own fault. You shouldn't have attacked," Halley had whispered to the mosquito-fairy, which was shaking its spike angrily at her. "You'll be OK here in the cupboard. You shouldn't even be hungry—you just ate. Take a nap or something."

Halley had closed the cupboard door but left a little opening for light. Even a mosquito-fairy probably hated the dark. A muffled *click-click-click* sounded from the cupboard. The mosquito-fairy was trying to break the thick glass with its sword-straw, but the jar was a fully secure fairy prison.

Then the monsters had immediately settled down. They stuffed themselves in the closet like the last time: first Grah flat against the back wall, then two more monsters with their big, hairy bellies pressed against each other, at most half of them inside the closet. Their heavy, matted heads were lowered on Grah's shoulders. In a moment, the whole monster threesome had dropped off.

Or pretended to have dropped off. Or something. Halley sighed, bored. Of all the things she was forced to think about. This was life with Mimi and Koby. They had to go on about things that didn't matter. Did the monster sleep or not? What did it matter? The fact was that the monster closed its eyes and stayed still for hours. It was all the same no matter what you wanted to call it.

Halley yawned. It was so boring. She was so awfully sleepy. From the bathroom came the hum of the hair dryer, Mimi's chattering, and Alice's giggling. The girls had washed the bathrobe and were now drying it with the hair dryer because Mimi wanted to wear it again. Wonder what Mom would say about that? One of Halley's eyes plopped shut by accident. She opened the eye quickly.

Muffled tinkling came from the kitchen. The angry spike fairy had not given up. And oh, how sleepy Halley was . . . What if she closed both eyes, just for a little moment? Oh, how lovely it felt. Would anyone care if Halley kept her eyes shut? The main thing was that somebody sat in front of the door. Nobody could open the door without Halley knowing. How blissful, lovely, sweet it was to sit here with her eyes closed, yet fully alert . . .

In less than a minute, Halley was fast asleep. After five minutes, she flopped to her side and drew herself into a ball on the hall rug like a guard dog—the difference being, of course, that she was not napping like a dog. She was in deep human sleep, and therefore noticed nothing when thick, bendy monster fingers grabbed her gently and picked her up off the floor. She merely sneezed sleepily when she was pressed against a dusty monster chest. Halley didn't even wake when she was put down clumsily in a strange, rustling place and covered up with something heavy. She wasn't even roused when the front door quietly clicked shut.

CHAPTER 17

The Monster's Natural Defense Mechanisms

MEANWHILE, ON THE BALCONY, Koby was reading Runar's book and was so immersed in it that he could almost hear Runar's voice in his ears. Koby was preparing for later that night. Everyone would naturally have questions, and Koby would be the only one who knew the answers. Or actually Runar. Runar and Koby together.

Koby turned first to Chapter 9 and started reading.

The Monster's Natural Enemies and Defense Mechanisms

The monster is strong and probably very scary in appearance to many people. When you have seen it charge and crash through a forest, you cannot believe that it would fear any other creature. The monster is clearly not a prey animal. It lacks the prey animal's sensitivity, which makes it run away at the slightest rustle. In any case, the monster itself causes plenty of noise. It would not survive a life-or-death fight, if something tried to hunt it.

But the monster is hardly a hunter either. It does not attempt to follow, scent, or find any living being. I never saw it chase or attack anything. On these grounds, I propose that the monster does not belong in any natural chain of predators and prey. So, is the monster an alien species in our forests?

Going around the forest with the monster, I noticed that it is wary of only one species: our own, the human. Whenever its keen senses detected a human being nearby, it tried to hide or leave the area. It is noteworthy that not even people who passed very closely noticed the monster. They looked directly at it, but could pass by without seeing the monster . . .

"Without seeing the monster," Koby repeated. He read on.

I did not manage to witness very many encounters between a human and monster (excepting my own) in our two years together. Indeed, one of the monster's means of survival may be disappearing or hiding.

On many occasions, I saw the monster become frightened or annoyed by something. Then it growled,

even roared, and flexed its muscles under its dusty coat
to create a strong smell of an earth cellar. But not once
did I get to see it defend itself or attack. Nevertheless,
my imagination tells me that in the case of the monster,
this would be a most interesting phenomenon. However,
I leave the study of this issue to the scientists of the
future. I had no opportunity to study it.

Koby nodded solemnly. Yes. He accepted the task. It
was self-evident that he, Koby Hellman, was one of the
future scientists about whom Runar wrote. The task had
already begun. Today Koby had seen the monster's defen-
sive smoke bomb. He had also seen the monster's enemy
and put it in a cookie jar. Actually, Halley had, but it was
in the jar now all the same. Koby had also examined the
fairy-frog's attack site on Minnie's monster's skin (a little
red dot, no visible injury, no evidence of pain at the sting
site).

Koby heard the hall phone ring inside the apartment.
Invisible Voice. He checked his watch. Almost seven. The
monsters must be awake by now and making supper.
Koby shut the book and hurried from the balcony into
the living room. There he saw, strangely enough, Halley
asleep on the trash bag–covered couch under the rag rug
usually kept at the hall door.

The phone continued to ring, and Koby went into
the hall. He instantly noticed that the closet door was

wide open. The closet was empty. Where were the monsters?

Koby grabbed the receiver and answered.

"Hello! Of course, the Hellmans. Hi, Dad, don't you recognize my voice? Koby here."

Koby looked around. At least one monster was still here, he noticed. Grah was sitting at the table between Mimi and Alice, drawing with colored pencils. They looked like tiny matchsticks in the monster's giant hands.

"What was that you said?" Koby asked, and concentrated on the call again. "What other way round?"

In the kitchen, Mimi whispered to Alice: "Maybe

Invisible Voice has found another way round the blizzard. I wonder how long it'll take to go around it?"

"When are you coming home?" Koby asked. "Why aren't you sure? Listen, if you arrive tonight, we may not be at home. Yes. No . . . listen. We're going on a night trip. I mean, a sleepover! That's what I meant. With Oscar and Minnie. Yes, well, you don't know our friends."

Koby listened to his father and answered: "Of course we'll take Mimi with us. Oscar has a little sister, too, Alice," Koby continued. "Yes, Alice is real. A real human, talks and everything."

"Dad thinks you're some imaginary friend! Even though I already told him the whole story," Mimi told Alice, giggling.

Koby went on: "Sure. In a tent in the yard. The tent was in our storage cage, it's quite OK. Oscar is a Boy Scout and knows all about camping. Yes, of course I do too!"

Mimi rolled her eyes, laughing. At best, Koby had watched camping shows on TV.

"Well, you can't know all our hobbies," Koby said kindly to the phone. "If we're not at home when you arrive, call my phone. Bye-bye!"

"Where *is* your dad?" Alice asked.

"A bit like a business trip and on the way home at the same time," Mimi said. "But now there's such a bad blizzard that the airport is closed, and he had to find another way round."

"Really, snow in June?" Alice queried.

Koby walked into the kitchen and asked: "Where are the other two monsters?"

"Looking for Oscar and Minnie, of course," Mimi replied. "Or maybe they didn't want to stay here anymore. With that."

Mimi pointed at the top cupboard, from where came an endless, muffled *click-click-click*. Koby nodded.

"What are you doing, by the way?" he asked.

"Watching Grah draw," Mimi said. Grah raised its head and grunted. Mimi stroked its back encouragingly.

"Well done, Grah!"

"It does break quite a few pencils," Alice said, eyeing the pile of broken pencils on the table.

"It can't help it," Mimi said. "It's only just learning to draw with colored pencils. Perhaps they're thicker wherever it came from. At its home."

Grah's home, thought Koby. *Wonder where it is?*

"What is it drawing?" he asked.

"Hard to tell," Mimi said, bending thoughtfully over Grah's drawing. "It's got a lot of green and black."

"And holes," Alice pointed with her finger.

"The holes aren't meant to be there," Mimi corrected Alice. "It just has thicker paper at home. It's used to paper that the pencil doesn't go through so easily."

"How do you know it has paper at home?" Koby asked.

"I have a feeling," Mimi answered evenly.

Grah moved restlessly. Perhaps it didn't want to think about the paper at home.

"It looks a bit like a forest to me," Koby said. "There are trees and some rocks. That black lump must be a mountain."

"It's a really nice picture, Grah." Mimi nodded approvingly. "What is that at the front?"

In the middle of the wild, messy, and holey drawing, there seemed to be a group of dark figures. Were they monsters? Could be. At least, they had huge hands. In front of them were three smaller . . . somethings. What were they? They were not monsters, because they were blond and multicolored.

"Grah, what are those?" Mimi asked, pointing at the colorful figures. Grah did not answer, just gazed at Mimi with its motionless globular eyes.

"Maybe it doesn't want to say," Alice mumbled.

"You don't have to say," Mimi said, patting Grah's arm.

"I could take that drawing and study it a little," Koby said, and reached for the paper. "I thought—"

He could say no more, because Grah's shovel palm slapped the drawing back on the table. Then the monster, eyes fixed on the table, screwed up the picture into a tiny crumpled ball.

"Oops," Koby managed to say. Mimi stroked the monster's back protectively.

"It's something personal, don't you see? Even monsters are allowed to have secrets," she muttered to Koby.

CHAPTER 18

The First Night in the Yard

AN EARLY SUMMER'S NIGHT in Finland is not dark. The air just gradually becomes heavier and more mystifying. The day birds stop their jolly twittering and fall asleep on their perches. The night birds open their beaks, but they do not twitter joyfully. They let out their strange, curious calls, as if to ask: *Is there anybody else here? Am I the only one awake?*

On this night the night birds were not alone. The grass playing field next to the marina had sprouted two tents: one for Halley, Mimi, Minnie, and Alice, the other for Koby and Oscar. Putting them up had been tricky; nevertheless, there they were, the first, slightly wonky dwellings of the monster camp. Right behind the tents was a small, dense forest, suitable for monster outings.

The other kids arrived at nine. Fourteen children had

had monsters sent to their homes. Fourteen! There were more of them than Koby had expected. They all talked at the same time, asking questions: What were the monsters? Where had they come from? Where did they go to the bathroom? How well did they understand speech? Why did they shed such enormous amounts of dust? Why did everybody think that they didn't exist? Why were the children not allowed to tell anyone about them? Were they really not dangerous, in spite of the growling?

Koby looked around and took a deep breath, strangely calm and excited at the same time. Nobody had told the new kids that Koby was the camp's monster expert. Yet they had all come straight to him. How had they known? Did it show somehow?

On the ground next to Koby stood a paper bag, from which a slow *click-click-click* came every now and then. The blocked view seemed to calm the fairy-troll. If it saw nobody, there was no need for it to be on the attack the whole time.

Koby scanned the edges of the field and the shadows under the trees. There was no sign of the monsters. They had not come with their children. Where were they?

"Are you really going to sleep out here?" asked Leo, Koby's classmate, who was looking at the tents behind Koby.

Koby nodded.

"At least tonight."

"Why?" asked Elijah, a blond-haired boy from another class at school. His little brother, Luke, was yawning next to him.

"We'll talk about that soon," Koby answered. "Does anybody know where their monsters are?"

"I bet our monster is at home, sleeping in the hall closet," said Jenna, who was in Minnie's class. Her sister, Alba, nodded in agreement.

"In the hall closet? How can it fit in there?" Leo asked.

"That's where ours stays, too," Elijah said.

"Where else could it be, anyway?" Alba asked.

"I suppose any place it can fit," Koby said. "Where does yours stay, Leo?"

"The shower stall. We haven't got a hall closet," Leo replied.

"So how do you take a shower?" Jenna asked.

Leo grinned.

"I don't shower."

"Yuck." Mimi sniffed.

"It has to let you take a shower — it's your nanny, after all," Halley insisted. Leo shrugged.

"It's a little bit kind of . . . grumpy. It growls if I go anywhere near the bathroom."

"Growls?" Jenna repeated, shocked. "Our monster never growls."

"It doesn't do anything if I don't go too close," Leo assured them. "In our building, we have a bathroom in the sauna, so I use that. I just need to take the elevator downstairs every time. It's a bit of a pain."

Jemima, a girl with long black braids, shook her head in sympathy. Oscar's blond friend Aron told them: "Ours wants to be in the same room as me all the time. It doesn't growl or make any noise; it just stares. I have to tell it to get into the closet after a while."

Minnie tittered.

"It's not funny," the boy said.

"Ours just stares at the TV," Luke said. "Any old program. It stayed behind to watch ballroom dancing. Every so often it drags itself into the kitchen and cooks us revolting potatoes with black spots. They get coated with that disgusting dust from its hands. And the minute the potatoes are done, it goes back to the TV."

"You eat nothing but potatoes?" asked Minnie.

"Potatoes and ketchup, many times a day," said Luke and Elijah.

"Yuck!" yelled Mimi. "Lucky our Grah knows how to make sandwiches and cocoa!"

"Did you give it a name?" Elijah asked.

"It already had a name," Mimi said mysteriously. "But Grah doesn't want anybody to know. Don't tell anyone."

"How did it tell you its name? Can it talk?" Luke asked.

"You can learn to understand it if you try a little," Mimi said.

A loud shushing sound came from the forest and made the children jump. A sudden gust of wind stirred the tree-tops and then faded.

"Strange wind," Halley said, peering into the forest.

"Monster wind," Mimi whispered to Alice with a grin. "It comes from many monsters running really fast in the forest." Alice wrapped herself tighter in her blanket.

"Aw, look at you, big baby," Halley said.

"The monsters don't want to harm us. They are our nannies, after all," Koby said calmly, even though his heart was also thrashing wildly, and his eyes kept flicking toward the forest shadows. "Have you fed your monsters?"

"Should we feed it?" Luke asked. "We were told that it takes care of its own food."

"Yes, it does," Koby began. "But you must help it a little. It needs to be let out to look for food. It can't find food inside, only in the forest."

"But it won't go outside!" the messy-haired boy sitting next to Oscar grumbled.

"Ours won't either. It just stares at the TV," Luke said.

"Or growls in the shower," Leo added.

Mimi started to giggle. "You pea brains! You need to go with it, of course. That's what we did. It can't go out on its own!"

"How did you work that out?" Leo asked. "Our instructions said nothing like that."

"We have additional information," Koby said grandly,

and held up Runar's book. "Look at this: a scientific book of monsters. We read in this book that the monster must be taken outside to eat."

"Really?" Elijah asked suspiciously.

"Where did you get it?" Alba wondered.

"The library," Koby replied, and Halley nodded.

"So what else does it say, then?" asked the girl with the black braids.

"It has loads of information, and I've only had time to read a bit of it. But you can look things up in it. What would you like to know?"

"Are monsters dangerous?" Alba asked instantly.

Koby didn't need to open the book to answer that question.

"They are not dangerous. But you must treat them well. You need to allow them to eat. And for that they must be taken to a forest."

"Why can't they go to eat on their own?" Alba asked.

"I don't know. Perhaps they need our permission. Or maybe they're not allowed to leave us alone," Koby replied pensively.

"But we're alone now," Minnie said in a small voice.

"Are you quite sure?" Mimi asked ominously, and laughed happily at Minnie's startled expression.

"We left home ourselves," Koby reminded her. "The monsters didn't leave us, we left them alone while they slept."

"But monsters don't sleep!" Mimi insisted. "They knew very well that we left!"

"Mimi, please don't keep on saying that!" Halley snapped irritably.

"Should we go get them? They can't eat if they're at home," Leo said.

"I'm pretty sure they'll come of their own accord," Koby said. "All we need to do is wait, and they'll find us. It's their job. And as soon as they're here, we'll take them to eat."

The children fell quiet and looked around. The forest behind the tents was all dark duskiness and night shadows. The thought of monsters who were probably looking for them right now was . . . well.

"Look," Halley whispered tremulously, pointing in the direction of the marina. "They already found us."

In the shadow of the great weeping willows on the other side of the playing field stood a dark, motionless group of monsters. They would have blended in with the gloom under the trees, but their eyes glowed like yellow Christmas lights. They stared at the children across the field. They might have been there for some time, watching the children holding their monster meeting.

"See, they knew where we were all the time," Mimi said to Halley. "They just decided to join us now."

Halley gulped with fright. Oscar hid behind Halley's back. Mimi took Alice's hand—Alice was trembling with

either fear or the evening coolness—and slipped her other hand in her bathrobe pocket. Koby closed the book and stood up, his heart pounding in his chest.

"Remember. There's no need to be afraid of them," Koby repeated, as much to himself as the others.

"Of course not!" Mimi piped up. "At least Grah is really nice."

"My monster is not nice," Leo said in a low voice.

"But surely it won't attack anybody?" Halley said sharply. "We're not in your shower stall now."

Halley was always a little argumentative when scared.

"They're coming this way," Oscar whispered.

He was right. The monster pack was on the move. They approached the camp slowly, almost as if they were floating above the field. How did such huge creatures manage to move so silently?

"Their intention is to take care of us," Koby assured everyone calmly, even though his heart was banging in his chest and his palms were sweating so much he could barely keep hold of Runar's book.

"What do we do now?" Oscar asked, alarmed.

Koby forced his voice to keep steady when he answered: "We'll go into the forest with them. We'll take them to eat. Just like we planned. You'll soon see how monsters live when they're not stuffed into closets."

"How could we possibly take them anywhere? I don't think they would obey us," Elijah said, worried.

"Perhaps not obey, but they will follow," Koby said. "We'll just walk into the forest and they'll follow us. Come on."

Koby turned and started to walk toward the woods behind the tents. The others stared at his back, aghast. How did he dare turn his back on the approaching monsters?

Koby stopped and looked over his shoulder.

"Well, are you coming or not?" he said.

The monster front was already gliding halfway across the field. Every moment brought them closer.

"Let's go," Leo said quickly. "Come on."

In three seconds, they were on their feet. First the children disappeared into the forest and then the monsters.

A couple of hours later, a rambunctious gang of kids, all talking and laughing at the same time, emerged from the forest. They had left the monsters happily in the forest, the monsters having eaten their fill of all kinds of half-rotted and disgusting things.

"They were like tanks, with trees crashing around them!" Aron said, laughing.

"Did you see the one lying in that muddy ditch?" Minnie giggled. "I hope it was Leo's monster—he can wash it in the shower."

"It wasn't mine," Leo said. "My monster sat in that

rock hollow—did you see? It was stuffing itself with both hands on dead twigs and rotten mushrooms."

"Can we take them to eat every night?" Alba asked hopefully. "And can we move out here too? If we bring our own tent?"

"Sure," Koby answered.

"We don't have a tent," Jemima said.

"There's room for you and Anna in our tent," Alba said.

"Leo, you can come with us in our tent, if you want," Elijah said.

"Thanks! And we can all use our bathroom and shower. I live very near here," Leo added.

"Can we leave the monsters out there in the forest?" Alba asked Koby, and yawned. It was almost midnight.

"They know how to follow us," Koby replied. "Like they did here."

"How long do they sleep after eating?" Jemima asked.

Koby thought for a minute.

"Grah always wakes up when it hears our voices," he said. "Perhaps you should set off on your bikes and talk in loud voices while pedaling. Monsters have very sharp hearing."

Anna and Jemima yawned.

"We'll try it. We can leave the door open so it can get in. See you tomorrow!" Anna said.

The girls had gotten halfway across the playing field

on their bikes, when a dark creature rushed out of the shadows of the forest. It caught up with the bikes in a few seconds and started jogging behind them. The girls noticed nothing.

"Wild," Halley said.

"They'll notice when they get home," Koby said, yawning.

"Let's go to bed," Oscar suggested.

"Let's," Koby said, and waved his hand to the children who weren't sleeping in a tent and were wandering off in different directions on their bikes and scooters, all heading for their homes. Nobody was scared anymore, the dusky night no longer ominous. Sudden rustlings were heard here and there in the forest as the monsters awoke and set off jogging after the children in their care.

CHAPTER 19

Camping Life

THE SUN WAS ALREADY shining high in the sky when Halley was awakened by the bleep of a text message arriving. She sat up and fumbled for her phone. The message was from Mom.

> Hi, darlings! Sun shining here. Awful lot of mosquitoes. How are you doing? Remember to play outdoors. Love to Dad. Love from Mom, who misses you terribly

Halley decided to answer right away. She couldn't be bothered to consult Koby about what to say.

All good. We've been
outside a lot. On a picnic
right now and having
lunch soon. Bye-bye!
Halley

The message went on its way, and Halley slipped out of her sleeping bag. She unzipped the tent door flap and crawled outside. The sun blinded her, and the tent village around her was teeming with life.

"Oh wow," Halley muttered, surprised.

Two new tents had appeared in the row, and a couple of Oscar's friends were just putting up a third. Kids were all over the place.

"Good morning," Koby greeted her in front of his tent, where he sat with Leo. "You woke up just at the right time!"

"What do you mean?" Halley asked, squinting.

"Someone has to go home to answer the phone when Invisible Voice calls at two. I thought it could be you."

"Two? What time is it?" Halley asked.

Koby glanced at his watch. "Almost one."

"Did I sleep until one?" Halley was aghast.

"Looks like it," Leo said.

"Do we have anything to eat?" Halley asked.

"We do," Koby said, pointing at an old cooler.

"What are you grinning at?" Halley asked, suspicious.

"Nothing," Leo said. "Get something to eat."

Halley sauntered over to the cooler and lifted the lid.

"What the heck?" slipped out of her mouth. The box was stacked full of sandwiches. No ordinary sandwiches, but sandwiches the size of a whole loaf, with twenty layers. Tottering, overfilled sandwiches, oozing with lettuce leaves and cheese slices, strawberry jam and salami, and—just a minute—was that a doughnut?

"There are some mugs of cocoa left in that basket, if you want some," Koby said. "Although they've been out for many hours now, might not be worth drinking."

Halley's eyes turned to the basket next to the cooler. On the bottom, in a large pool of cocoa, sat half a dozen mugs full of familiar-looking, almost solid cocoa.

"Grah has made breakfast," Halley said.

"Not just Grah," Koby said. "Have a look in the sauce-pan next to it."

Halley lifted the lid off the saucepan that was sitting in the grass.

"Revolting," Halley groaned. The pan was full of unpeeled potatoes with black spots and copious amounts of ketchup squirted on top.

Koby grinned.

"The pan appeared soon after Luke and Elijah put their tent up."

"What do you mean, 'appeared'? Where are the monsters?" Halley asked.

"Probably someplace not far away," Koby said, looking around. "Maybe they don't like daylight. I'm sure they'll turn up again in the evening."

"Some nannies we've got there." Halley smiled and carefully helped herself to the top layer of a tottering bread skyscraper. Egg and strawberry jam, not a bad combination. But the mustard might have been better left out.

"What shall I tell Invisible Voice?" Halley asked, munching on her sandwich.

"The most important thing is to find out when he intends to become visible," Koby said.

Leo threw a questioning look at Koby.

"In other words, come home," Halley explained,

taking a bite of her sandwich. Mmm, was there some anchovy paste in it too?

Leo nodded slowly.

When Halley returned to the camp a few hours later, there were two more tents. Someone had spread blankets on the grass; someone else had brought a couple of patio chairs from home. A few kids were playing soccer. Koby stood on the edge of the playing field, clutching Runar's book to his chest.

Halley stopped next to Koby.

"What's wrong?" she asked her brother.

"I was just thinking whether setting up camp just anywhere is allowed."

Halley frowned.

"This isn't anybody's yard. The tents don't bother anyone here."

"Maybe not," Koby said, eyeing the row of tents. "But there are special camping sites. They wouldn't exist if everybody were allowed to go camping wherever they liked."

"Bah," Halley said dismissively. "These are special circumstances. In special circumstances, anything is allowed."

Koby did not look convinced.

"What did Invisible Voice say?" he asked.

"Nothing. Because he never called at all," Halley replied.

"Are you sure the phone was plugged in?"

"Of course it was, stupid," Halley grumbled.

"Just asking," Koby said. "That could mean that he really is on his way and he'll be here soon."

"Or else the phone lines have frozen and snapped. Or the phone exploded in the blizzard. Something like that." Halley grinned.

Koby was not laughing. He looked even more worried.

Little by little, the sun wandered westward, the light turned more orange, and the air began to have a scent of evening. The first camping day had been brilliant: The picnic food had lasted all day. The monsters had kept well out of sight. But the closer evening came, the more the children began to expect the monsters. When would they come, and from which direction this time?

Koby got a blanket and spread it on the ground in front of his tent. Halley and Leo sat down next to him. Jenna and Alba were lying half inside their tent, half out, listening to music on one earbud each.

"Tea for everybody who wants some, bring your own mugs," Elijah announced from his camping stove.

Leo turned to Koby and asked: "So why did you decide to start living in tents?"

Halley and Koby exchanged a glance.

"It's easier to take the monsters out," Halley began.

"And to be honest, we received a hint that it was best to leave," Koby continued.

"What do you mean, 'best'?" Leo asked.

"Safest and easiest," Halley explained, giving Koby a warning look. They didn't need to share any of Mimi's bathrobe stories right now.

"We received a hint that there may be other beings at large, apart from monsters," Koby went on uncertainly, eyeing Halley back.

"Like what other beings?" Jenna asked, sitting up. She looked concerned.

"Was it in that old book?" Leo asked.

"Well, not exactly," Koby began, but got no further, as Mimi stuck her head out of her tent and interrupted Koby, proudly declaring:

"My bathrobe told us. This one here!"

Mimi patted her blue bathrobe. Halley shut her eyes. The game was lost. All the kids would know that her muddle-headed little sister imagined that she talked to a bathrobe.

Next to Mimi, Alice was nodding emphatically.

"It's alive. I saw it."

"A bathrobe that's alive?" Leo repeated, giving Koby a puzzled look. His voice had laughter in it. Koby looked very embarrassed.

"The bathrobe is kind of . . . Mimi's imaginary friend," Koby said, throwing Mimi a warning glance. He knew he wasn't telling the truth, but it was time for Mimi to learn that she could not talk about the bathrobe just anywhere. Mimi's bathrobe was a family secret. You didn't tell everybody about it.

"What are you rabbiting on about!" Mimi yelled, insulted. "Don't lie! Numskull! You've seen it yourself many times!"

Halley was seething with anger. She was so fed up with the whole stupid bathrobe thing!

"Mimi made the whole story up—anybody can see that. Or have you ever heard of talking bathrobes? She is just so babyish," Halley huffed.

"It's not true! Don't lie!" Mimi screamed, her little hands squeezed into tight fists. "Koby! Tell the truth! Don't be a wimp!"

Koby was very uncomfortable. He eyed Mimi sternly and said: "Please don't yell, Mimi. That bathrobe *is* rather a strange business—"

"It is NOT a strange business!" Mimi bellowed, stamping her foot. "The strange business is that you haven't got the guts to admit that you've seen it yourself. You big chicken licken! You don't deserve the bathrobe's help! I'm leaving—you can manage without me and the bathrobe. Alice, come!"

Mimi stormed off toward the forest, the frightened

Alice in tow. Koby looked at Halley miserably. He hadn't guessed that Mimi would get so upset. The other kids looked wide-eyed between Koby and Halley, and at Mimi and Alice getting farther and farther away.

"Bah, let them go," Halley asserted. "They'll be back soon. Really, think about it: a talking bathrobe. Stark barking bonkers."

Leo, Alba, and Jenna chuckled uncertainly. It did sound stark barking bonkers.

But Koby looked miserable. He had a guilty conscience.

"Where were we?" he mumbled.

"The hints and other beings," Jenna said.

Koby nodded. He picked up the cookie jar in the paper bag off the grass. No sounds came from the jar anymore; it had been quiet all day. That worried Koby a little. What if the fairy-troll was dead?

"I wanted to show you this," Koby said, taking the jar from the bag. He lifted the jar up in the air for the others to see.

"What is that?" asked Alba, amazed.

"All I know is that it's an enemy of the monsters. Halley caught it in a net. It had gotten inside our apartment and attacked Minnie's monster," Koby said.

"So little and it attacked a monster!" Oscar marveled.

"Is it dead?" Luke asked.

"Don't think so," Koby said, worried. "Maybe it's just sleeping."

He shook the jar gently, but the creature stayed still. Halley and Mimi had slipped some cotton balls into the jar the day before, for padding, and the critter had fashioned them into a round nest. Then it had rolled itself into a ball in its nest like a tiny cat. Its bulldog face was hidden. Its spiky straw was held tightly in one hand.

"It may be hungry," Halley said. "It's had nothing to eat since yesterday."

"What could we give it?" Koby asked. "We don't have any monster blood."

"Yuck, does it eat monster blood?" Jenna asked. Alba wrinkled her nose.

"It also eats candy," Halley said.

"I've got some toffee in my pocket," Alba said. "Would that do?"

"We could try it," Koby said.

Alba handed him a piece of toffee. Koby unscrewed the lid carefully. It was possible that the creature was pretending. Maybe it was just waiting for the lid to open slightly so it could bolt out and into freedom. But the fairy lay motionless. Koby dropped the piece of toffee. It clunked on the bottom, but the mosquito-fairy didn't even stir.

"What if it needs water?" Luke suggested.

"Let's try," Koby said.

They drizzled a few drops out of Luke's water bottle. The fairy still didn't move. Koby closed the lid.

"I hope it's not dead," he said, feeling wretched.

"I'm sure it's just asleep," Halley said. "It'll wake up again soon."

"Perhaps," Koby said, defeated.

"We should eat something too," Halley said. "With a bit of luck, we'll have time before the monsters bring us their delicacies."

But that night the monsters stayed away. The children saw neither hide nor hair nor shadow of them. Not a rustle came from the forest. No black-spotted potatoes came, no sandwiches, nothing. There was no sign of the monsters, and the forest was silent and empty.

"Maybe they don't eat every night," Koby said finally, when everybody was too tired to wait anymore.

"They'll be in trouble now," Halley mumbled sleepily.

"How so?" Koby asked.

"They're supposed to take care of us, and they didn't even bring us food," Halley said, yawning. "Whoever sent them can't be happy."

Koby nodded. Halley was right. The monsters had forgotten the children in their care.

Gradually, the camp went quiet. One after another, the kids crawled into their tents and fell asleep without supper.

Only Koby stayed awake, thinking. He couldn't sleep. Where were Mimi and Alice? Why had the monsters not come? What had happened to the fairy? Was all this somehow Koby's fault?

CHAPTER 20

The Bathrobe's Advice

I'VE NEVER HAD a bath so late before," Mimi said, diving into the warm bubbles. Alice yawned and sat down on the toilet lid.

"Don't sit there," Mimi said. "That's the bathrobe's place. Let's keep very quiet and maybe it'll wake up again."

There was a scent of apple bath bubbles in the bathroom. Alice sat down on the cold floor after putting the bathrobe in her spot. They watched as it sprawled lifelessly on the toilet lid. Minutes passed. Nothing happened.

"Alice," Mimi said pensively.

"Yes?"

"Perhaps it's scared of you. Would you go somewhere else for a while?"

"Like where?" Alice asked in a very small voice. She didn't like being alone.

"Like the kitchen. I'll call you back in a minute."

Alice stood up uncertainly and took a few steps toward the door.

"Go on," Mimi said, shooing her.

Alice sighed.

"Shall I close the door?" she asked in her small voice as she left. Mimi didn't answer.

"Mimi?"

"Come back in after all," Mimi said, her voice trembling with excitement. "It woke up!"

Alice turned back and gasped with amazement. The bathrobe sat, charmingly lively, on the toilet lid. The sleeves gestured with speech, although there was no sound.

Alice watched Mimi. Mimi was laughing at something the bathrobe was saying. If Alice could have heard the conversation going on in front of her eyes, she would have heard this:

Mimi (relieved): So, you woke up at last!

Bathrobe: Hee-hee!

Mimi: What are you laughing at?

Bathrobe: You've dragged me around to some pretty strange places. You should remember that I am a bathrobe, after all. Not a forest picnic robe. Or basement robe!

Mimi: I wanted to keep you with me all the time.

Bathrobe: Hee-hee!

Mimi: I even know how to use the washing machine now!

Bathrobe: I should know. I'm the one who was in the washing machine.

Mimi: Sorry. You were filthy.

Bathrobe: It's OK. It had to be done. Well, what did you want to ask me?

Mimi: How did you know that I want to ask you something?

Bathrobe: Well, it's pretty obvious. Let's hear it. We may be interrupted.

Mimi: What do you mean, 'interrupted'?

Bathrobe: I mean that if you don't ask now, there will be no time soon.

Mimi: I see. Well. Last time you said that there were others on the move, apart from monsters. Did you mean the flying spike fairy?

Bathrobe: Probably.

Mimi: Are there still others?

Bathrobe: Well . . . next question!

Mimi: You are so infuriating!

Bathrobe: Perhaps I am. Next question!

Mimi: What was the third hint that you didn't have time to give me last time?

The bathrobe settled itself in a more comfortable position, as if it was about to tell her a long story.

Bathrobe: The third hint was that monsters live in a different way from you humans. They have no families; they have chains.

Mimi: What do you mean, 'chains'? Some jewelry, you mean?

Bathrobe: Not jewelry. Listen now. They have monster chains. Each monster has its place in the chain, and they can't take any other monster's place. In a way, they are all joined to one another, just like the links in a chain. If you draw one monster to you, you gradually draw them all.

Mimi: I don't get it at all. They're not joined together in any way.

The bathrobe chuckled lightly.

Bathrobe: Of course you don't get it! You are . . . (thoughtful pause)

Mimi: What am I?

Bathrobe: You are a human child.

Mimi: So I am!

Bathrobe: So you are. That is why I chose you.

Mimi: How do you mean, 'chose'? You're Koby's old bathrobe, and as far as I know, Mom chose you at the store.

Bathrobe: As far as you know.

Mimi: Now I'm getting mad!

Bathrobe: Not yet. I'm not finished.

Mimi: Yes, monsters have chains.

Bathrobe: Right. Now concentrate.

Mimi: Tell me!

Bathrobe: Patience. Try to focus. So, monsters have a kind of standing order. Or walking order. Even if they go far away from each other, they must come back to their own place. Do you understand, little friend?

Mimi: No.

Bathrobe: What is it you don't understand?

Mimi: I've seen loads and loads of monsters, and they never stand in any order. And they never come back from anywhere.

Bathrobe: Are you quite sure?

Mimi: Why wouldn't I be?

Bathrobe: Do you know where they are right now?

Mimi: Probably running around the forest.

Bathrobe: Well. They are not.

Mimi: Where are they, then?

Bathrobe: They are looking for each other.

Mimi: Why?

Bathrobe: If one of their family chain has come to the humans' world, the others must come after it. They can't get back to their home until all of them are together. One of them is missing. And yes, maybe somebody wants to stop them from getting back home.

Mimi: That's crazy!

Bathrobe: Oh well. To each his own. There are always bad creatures as well as good ones.

Mimi: Monsters are not bad!

Bathrobe: Did I say that monsters are bad? I don't think so.

Mimi thought for a moment before going on.

Mimi: Do they want to go back to . . . er, wherever they came from?

Bathrobe: Naturally. Everybody wants to go back home. They don't really fit in here. They shed too much of that dust. And anyway, people are afraid of them.

Mimi: True.

Bathrobe: And people usually start to tease and bully anybody who is different.

Mimi: Yuck, that is so mean.

Bathrobe: You have a monster too.

Mimi: But it's really nice. And we don't bully it!

Bathrobe: What do you think: does it prefer your hall closet to its own home?

Mimi: What?

Bathrobe: You heard me.

For a moment, Mimi was quiet and seemed to be at a loss. Then she asked hesitantly: "Do you have a home somewhere too?"

The bathrobe burst out in laughter.

"Of course not! I am a bathrobe! But a monster is a monster, not a nanny. Understand?"

"I understand," Mimi said.

They were silent for a moment.

> **Mimi:** So, where is the monster that's missing from the chain?
>
> **Bathrobe:** Ah, yes! Do I know the answer to everything? Maybe I do, maybe I don't. In any case, I can give you this advice: Use your head! You have all the information you need. And here comes the final extra hint: Look under Koby's arm.
>
> **Mimi:** Under Koby's arm! Have you gone crazy?
>
> **Bathrobe:** The interruption is coming.
>
> **Mimi:** What?
>
> **Bathrobe:** I told you there would be an interruption soon. Mimi! You can solve this! I did not choose you by mistake. Take care of Alice.

At that very moment, a key turned in the front door. Alice let out a frightened squeal. The bathrobe flopped limply on the toilet lid and slid in a blue bundle to the bathroom floor.

"Yoo-hoo, anybody home?" came a familiar voice from the hall. "Koby? Halley? Mimi? Are you in bed already?"

"Who is that?" Alice whispered to Mimi, alarmed.

"It's my dad," Mimi replied, surprised. "Invisible Voice."

"Why does he come home in the middle of the night?" Alice whispered.

"He's been in a blizzard and had to take an alternative route," Mimi said, and called: "Dad! I'm in here, in the bath!"

CHAPTER 21

The Angry Newborn

MEANWHILE, IN THE CAMP, Koby dropped off to sleep for a while but then woke up again. He lay in the dark tent, shivered a little, and considered the situation. Next to him, Oscar was snuffling in his sleep. Koby tried to find an even vaguely comfortable position on the thin camping mattress. He was worried about Mimi and Alice. The worry was a pressure like a pinecone beneath him. He did know that Mimi could take care of herself. She and Alice had probably gone home. Grah was likely to be with them. But still. Mom would not like this.

For a moment, Koby considered going home, but he couldn't leave the camp without telling anyone. Best to wait until sunrise. Which would happen soon. One of the advantages of Nordic summer nights.

In addition to his worries, Koby was utterly disappointed. He had been quite certain the monsters would come back. Where on earth were they? Why had they not returned last night? Their job was to stay close to the children. Everything had gone just as Koby had thought it would, until suddenly everything had started to go completely wrong. Koby's first monster theory had been ruined, and he couldn't stop turning the matter over and over in his mind. Which bit had he misunderstood? Which, which, which?

Sleep just wasn't happening. He sat up and dug a flashlight out of his rucksack. He rolled up a blanket under his arm, picked up Runar's book, and crept out of the tent. Outside, he wrapped the blanket tightly around himself and sat down on the dewy grass. It was silent, lonely, and cool. It was the moment closest to darkness on a summer's evening. Koby looked around, and the night stared back at him. *Why did you come here, what for?* the night seemed to be asking.

Koby had nothing to say to the night. He pulled the blanket over his head to make his own little tent, clicked the flashlight on, and opened Runar's book to the table of contents. His eyes stopped at the chapter title "The Monster's Human-like Habits." Were there some? Koby leafed through to the correct page number and realized immediately that the chapter was particularly short. Interesting. He began to read.

It is indisputable, even abundantly clear, that the monster resembles humans to a degree. Its appearance points to primates: the coat, strength, certain animal behavior, more on which in the next chapter. In terms of its mental faculties — one could say spiritual qualities — however, the monster is undoubtedly closer to humans than chimpanzees.

As I write this, the psychology of the monster is naturally still a mystery in many ways. It cannot describe it itself, at least not in any language we understand. Does it speak some other language, one of its own? Do monsters have their own culture, even their own works of art or beliefs? In my view it is possible, even likely. The monster's mental faculties are sufficient.

It is also evident that the monster is capable of interaction with humans. It is capable of cooperation. On the other hand, it has emotional weaknesses that are also typical of humans: the monster may feel upset, become bitter or even vengeful. It remembers the good and bad things it has experienced for a long time. It clearly likes some people more than others. As an example, I may cite the case of the new housekeeper I related before, which could have had a very sorry ending had I not intervened.

The monster easily learns to understand human speech. Based on my own experience, though it is limited, I would say that the language skills achieved by the monster are of a sufficient level for it to live in the human world. The monster also learns easily to do many of the jobs in the human world. For example, in farming or gardening, these strong and tenacious creatures could be a great help to humans.

However, the crucial question could be whether or not monsters themselves have any natural need or desire for it. Given the choice of company and habitat, it would hardly choose coexistence with humans. The disparity between the two species is too great. An equal environment would not be possible. The monster would not choose to be slave labor for humans. Regular human work would be alien to its free, wild nature.

Slave labor! Koby stopped reading. Had Grah been forced to come to them against its will? But who could force monsters into anything? Every monster had the strength of at least ten humans, and monsters were not afraid of anything. Except perhaps that spike fairy creature.

Koby's eyes scanned the next chapter title: "The Monster's Animal-like Habits." This chapter was considerably longer, many pages of dense text without any pictures. Reading by flashlight made his eyes tired. Koby closed his eyes and thought of perhaps trying to sleep a little after all.

Suddenly he heard a strange noise coming from somewhere nearby. Koby opened his eyes and listened. It was a very small, scratchy, metallic sound. There was also slight rustling, barely discernible crackling, like thin ice cracking. Ice in June?

Koby switched off the flashlight and took the blanket off his head. There was the noise again, close. Then a new noise. A little bigger, a different clatter. Something fell down. Very close. Then, suddenly, the frightened, sleepy voice of Oscar from the tent: "Ouch! What was that? Koby, careful, that hurts! *Ahh!*"

"Oscar, I'm outside," Koby said, puzzled.

"Ow! Something bit me—are there bugs in here?" Oscar's frantic voice was accompanied by the sound of fierce sleeping-bag rustling.

Koby threw down his blanket, book, and flashlight. He grabbed the zipper on the tent flap and opened it with a quick tug. But before he had time to dive into the tent, something flew out the door. Oscar had thrown a sock at him!

Or not. Unlike a thrown rolled-up sock, this ball did not fall toward the ground. On the contrary, it rose higher and higher. *What on earth?* Koby managed to think, when the ball lit up. Then he knew.

"No!" he cried.

Suddenly the flying ball broke up into many small parts, as if exploding, and each little part lit up. One, two, three . . . Koby managed to count at least six before the flying dots of light vanished in the night sky.

Oscar's sleep-muddled head appeared in the tent doorway.

"What was it?" he asked, frightened, hair sticking up in all directions. "It bit me."

The door of the next tent opened, and Halley's head popped out.

"What are you yelling at?" she demanded.

"The fairy-frog escaped," Koby explained darkly. "Or fairy-frogs. There were at least six of them."

"What? Give me the flashlight," Halley said, crawling out of her tent.

Half a minute later, Halley had the spike fairy's empty cookie jar in one hand, the lid in the other.

"Look at this."

Halley shined the light at the inside of the lid. The underside was full of little gouged dents, circling the inside edge of the lid like a string of pearls.

"I thought it was just banging on the sides. It was much cleverer than I thought. Using those dents, it managed to unscrew the lid from below," Koby said, and took the lid from Halley to examine it more closely.

"What is that?" Oscar asked, pointing at little light-colored piles on the bottom of the jar, under the cottonball nest. Halley aimed the flashlight.

"Looks just like . . ." she began, puzzled, and bent closer.

"They look like eggshells," Koby said.

"Eggshells?" Oscar echoed. "How is that possible? The jar was closed all the time. How could some bird get in there to lay eggs?"

"Well, it couldn't, dumbo," Halley asserted. Silent and pondering, Koby stared at the eggshells on the bottom of the jar.

"I'm thinking . . ." he began, and fell silent again.

"What?" Halley asked.

Koby frowned and said: "What if these are its own eggshells?"

"Did anyone see eggs with it?" Halley was doubtful. "It was in a glass jar. A transparent glass jar."

"The jar was covered up all day," Koby said. "Last time we saw the mosquito-fairy, it was lying in a ball like a cat, not moving at all. Perhaps it was hatching the eggs."

Halley wrinkled her brow.

"Oh, so it would have laid eggs and hatched them at lightning speed in one night into babies?"

"It's possible," Koby said. "Maybe it already had the eggs in its pocket."

"In its pocket!" Halley scoffed. Of all the mad ideas.

"So are there lots more of them now?" Oscar was alarmed.

"Could be," Koby said, looking up at the blue-gray night sky. No more spots of light were flying anywhere.

"What if they attack us? What if they're angry because we put their mom in a jar?" Oscar asked quietly.

"Of course they won't attack us. They're monster mosquitoes. We're not monsters," Koby replied.

"It stung me," Oscar said.

"Self-defense," Koby said.

"What did I do to it? I was asleep," Oscar insisted.

Just then they heard it. A tiny, determined voice squeaked somewhere very close: *"Ah-ah-ah! Ee-ee-ee!"*

"Shhh," Halley hissed. "There's one more in here! We must find it."

Oscar was paralyzed on the spot.

"Ah-ah-ah!" the voice squeaked.

"Where is it?" Oscar began to panic.

"Ee-ee-ee!" came again.

"The sound is coming from the jar," Halley whispered. The fairy's cookie jar was still in her hand. "Quick! Where's the lid?"

The lid was in Koby's hand. He slammed it on the jar and screwed it tightly shut. Oscar sighed with relief.

"Look," Halley said. "Koby was right."

Halley shined the light in the jar. On the bottom, a tiny, partly split fairy egg had rolled from the ruins of the cotton-ball nest. It was pink and very small, and it cracked. The split opened up more. From the crack emerged a tiny greenish head, which stared at the children belligerently and squealed: *"Ah-ah-ah!"*

"A newly born monster mosquito," Koby whispered. "Incredible. Even Runar knew nothing about this."

"Why is it yelling so much?" Oscar asked. "The first one wasn't as cross as this."

"It may be missing its mom," Halley said. "Or it's hungry. I've heard that babies get cross if they're hungry."

"Should we feed it?" Oscar asked.

"Why not let it out of the jar and it can fly to the others?" Halley suggested.

"It won't find the others anymore," Koby said. "What on earth are we to do with it?"

CHAPTER 22

Mimi and Grah

THE BIRDS WERE TWITTERING their morning songs, and the sun was waking up the bumble-bees and other buzzing insects of a summer day. The grass behind the bush, under the balconies, was cool but suitably sheltered for Mimi and Grah. Ten o'clock in the morning was an unusual time to be out in the yard with a monster, even if they were partially hidden in a bush.

But they could not stay inside. Not now that Invisible Voice had become a visible Dad. He was sleeping soundly in his own bed, but it had been quite a job to get him to calm down and to believe that everything was fine. That there was a good reason why Alice and Mimi were home alone and Mimi was in the bath in the middle of the night. And that it was not at all terrible for Halley and Koby to be camping somewhere in the yard.

Grah had turned up at the door in the morning, at 6:12, to be precise. It had knocked very quietly, but Mimi had woken instantly and crept out to open the door.

"Good thing you didn't ring the bell," Mimi had whispered as Grah slipped straight into its closet. Maybe it was embarrassed. Or else just tired.

But now they were in the yard and the sun was shining. Mimi patted Grah's arm.

"Just try it," she coaxed. "You know how!"

Grah watched Mimi with its yellow eyes, a blank look on its face. Mimi sighed. She wanted Grah to show her how the invisibility dust worked. She wanted to see how the monster disappeared from sight, like Halley had said.

But Grah, who was usually so agreeable, wouldn't do anything at all.

"Mimi," came a tentative call from above.

A small blond head peeked over the balcony rail. It was Alice. She had stayed on Dad watch. Her job was to tell Mimi when Dad awoke.

"Is Dad awake?" Mimi asked.

"Not yet. Are you finished? Are you coming back in now?"

"Not just yet," Mimi said, frowning. "Grah is really stubborn today. It won't do anything."

Grah grunted.

"What do I say when your dad wakes up?" Alice said. "He's sure to ask me where you are. And why I'm at your house on my own."

"Tell him that I went out to the yard," Mimi said. "Go in now!"

"So you're allowed out in the yard alone, without telling anybody?" Alice went on up above.

"Course not, but Dad doesn't know that," Mimi answered. "I bet he can't even remember how old I am."

"Can I tell him if he asks?" Alice asked.

"Asks what?"

"Well, how old you are?"

"Oh, Alice! Go in now, I'm in the middle of something here," Mimi snapped.

Reluctantly, Alice vanished from the balcony. It was not always easy to be Mimi's helper.

Behind the bush, Mimi turned back to the monster, who was staring blankly at the forest.

"What are you thinking?" Mimi asked.

Grah's eyes moved so fast that only the end result of the motion was noticed: suddenly the eyes were no longer looking at the forest but were fixed on Mimi. Mimi recalled the bathrobe's words.

"Are you missing that . . . your own home?" she asked.

Grah stared at her, motionless.

"Where is your home?" Mimi went on.

Grah moved restlessly and turned to look back toward the forest.

"There in the woods?" Mimi asked. Grah said nothing, as usual.

"Don't you like staying with us?" Mimi asked. "I think it's nice to have you with us."

Grah looked at Mimi. Perhaps it did not want to answer.

"I feel silly talking to myself here," Mimi said. "I wish you would answer."

Grah stared.

"But I do understand." Mimi sighed. "I understand now that the bathrobe explained it. This is not your home. Everybody wants to go to their own home. You need to get back to your own home too."

Out of the blue, Grah put out its huge, thick-fingered hand and poked Mimi very gently in the cheek.

"Ouch," Mimi said, surprised.

Very slowly and carefully, Grah placed its hand against Mimi's cheek. Or actually against her head, because Mimi's head was quite small and Grah's hand was very big. Suddenly Mimi understood what the monster was doing: it was stroking her cheek!

"Aww." Mimi sighed and without a moment's hesitation threw herself into the monster's arms and hugged the thick, dusty, heavy monster as hard as she could.

"Oh, Grah! We can still be friends, even if our homes

are in different places! But how on earth can we find our way to your monster home? I don't know. But I'm sure we'll figure it out!"

Grah patted Mimi's hair fondly.

Suddenly there was the sound of shuffling. Someone was walking on the other side of the bush that Mimi and Grah were behind. Mimi let go of Grah and held her breath. Grah was quite still.

The ominous silence lasted a few seconds. Then it started: an awful yapping and roaring.

"It's Eric," Mimi whispered. "Perhaps he's on his own."

Of course Eric was not on his own. He was never on his own. Behind him Pattie Newhouse walked daintily in her fuchsia tracksuit, which made a swishing noise as she moved.

"Eric, be quiet," the lady shushed.

"Woof-woof-woof-woof-woof!" Eric roared.

"What's there in the bush? Can you smell a pussycat or a wee squirrel?" the lady chatted, stopping by the bush.

"Woof-woof-woof-woof-woof!" barked Eric.

"Go!" Mimi whispered to the monster.

She tried to nudge the monster to move, but Grah seemed bolted to the ground.

"Go on!" Mimi urged. "Run and hide!"

Grah bowed its head and began to shake, trembling from head to toe.

"Woof-woof-woof-woof-woof!" Eric barked on the other side of the bush.

"Shush now, boy," Mrs. Newhouse said, trying to calm him down.

Grah's ragged and matted coat began to emit dark

smoke in big swirls. The swirls quickly turned as transparent as air. Mimi watched, fascinated. It all happened with amazing speed.

"You can . . ." Mimi whispered. All she could see was green: forest, leaves, moss. Grah had disappeared from view, and not a moment too soon.

"Let's take a look, then, silly dog," said Mrs. Newhouse as she shoved a part of the bush aside. Mimi was staring straight at the lady's surprised blue eyes. Even Eric was surprised and stopped barking. Mimi did not dare to look to her side. She was afraid a bit of Grah, a toe or finger or something, was showing.

"Mimi, why are you sitting in a bush in your bathrobe?" the lady asked, puzzled.

"I am sitting behind the bush," Mimi answered haughtily. "It's nice and shady here. I'm studying beetles."

"Beetles, is it?" the lady said. "Are you all alone? Would you like me to take you home?"

"No, thank you," Mimi said. If only Mrs. Newhouse would be on her way quickly.

"Beetles are really easily frightened by dog barking," Mimi went on.

"Is that so? I didn't know that beetles have ears and everything!" the lady exclaimed, marveling at the notion.

"*Woof-woof-woof-woof-woof!*" Eric was off again.

"Eric, mind your muzzle, now—you'll frighten the beetles, did you hear? Shush, shush!" the lady scolded.

"What's the racket out here?" a sleepy shout came from up above. Invisible Voice—in other words, Dad—had woken up. Alice had not raised the alarm! Mimi frowned.

"Anything wrong?" Dad called. "The dog is barking so much that I can't sleep. Is Mimi there?"

"Here!" Mimi called back. "I'm studying nature."

"Woof-woof-woof!" called Eric.

"Eric, now shush once and for all!" Mrs. Newhouse told him sternly, and Eric finally stopped barking.

"Nature, is it," Dad said, scratching his head. "Good job. Are you coming in for breakfast soon? Alice seems to be here already."

"Quite soon," Mimi said. "Two minutes."

"Well, now, we must go and have our breakfast, too," Mrs. Newhouse said to Eric. "Bye-bye, everybody!"

Dad waved his hand and disappeared from the balcony. Silence fell in the bush. At last Mimi dared to look at the spot where Grah had sat. Nothing. The spot was empty.

Mimi screwed up her eyes and blew into the air. Nothing. She blew harder. The scenery began to quiver, just slightly, barely noticeably. Like the surface of water. You would not have noticed unless you were looking for it.

Mimi blew some more. The air moved, and the scenery folded like a curtain at the theater. There was a flash of something browny-black. A hairy arm!

"Grah!" Mimi sighed. "There you are."

The monster's arm waved in the air, first once and then many times. With each wave of its arm, the air moved aside and the monster gradually came into view. Finally it sat next to Mimi fully visible.

"You can, you can!" Mimi whispered excitedly, and clapped. Then she threw herself into the monster's lap and squeezed as hard as she could. The monster's huge chest echoed with something that sounded a bit like a giant cat purring.

CHAPTER 23

Where Are the Monsters?

MEANWHILE, IN THE MONSTER camp, Koby had just woken up and was sitting behind the tent, answering Mom's text messages, more of which were coming all the time. It had all begun well but quickly turned bad.

Mom, 9:35 a.m.:

> Morning, darlings! Hope
> I didn't wake you. When
> you go to bed early, you
> wake up early. It's so
> pretty and carefree here.
> Remember to get fresh
> air. How is it going with
> that creature?

Koby, 9:53 a.m.:

> You didn't wake us.
> Weather fine here. We
> are outside all the time.
> Would be nice if you
> came home.

Koby deleted the last sentence so that Mom wouldn't think she really should come home. "We miss you," he wrote instead. He sent the message. His tummy rumbled.

Mom, 10:06 a.m.:

> Koby, how are things
> *really* going there? One
> of the moms here said
> she got a message from
> her child saying that
> a big gang of children
> are living in tents in the
> yard with you. And that
> the creatures have gone
> away and you are there
> on your own. Is this
> true?

Koby, 10:07 a.m.:

> Ha-ha! Of course not. We
> do have tents set up but
> nobody LIVES in them.
> We're just playing. All is
> well! The monster must
> be at home with Mimi.

At least, that was what Koby hoped. In truth, he had no idea where Mimi was. The thought was stressful. Koby deleted the words "must be."

> The monster is at home
> with Mimi. Tell the other
> parents that all the kids
> are here playing with us.
> We'll have a picnic soon.
> Have a nice day.

His belly gurgled. If only they were having a picnic! But all the food was gone, Mimi and Alice were lost, and the monsters had run off. There was a cross mosquito-fairy baby in the cookie jar, for which they should find some food. When would he be forced to tell Mom the truth? *Bleep-bleep!* Another message.

Mom, 10:13 a.m.:

Good to hear! Called
home and they were
just having breakfast. All
sounds well. I just worry
when I can't see for
myself that everything is
OK. I should have known
that you are sensible
and reliable kids. Bye-
bye, Love, Mom

What on earth? Koby thought. Who had Mom spoken to? Mimi and Alice?

Tousled, sleepy kids were crawling out of the tents. Koby slipped the phone into his pocket.

"Where's breakfast?" Oscar asked Koby, and yawned.

"Haven't got any," Koby said. "The monsters haven't brought anything."

"Good." Luke was pleased. "No more potatoes!"

"What can we eat, then?" Jemima asked sleepily.

"We'll have to go home to eat. And to see if the monsters have gone there. We must find them," Koby said.

"Are they lost?" Halley asked. "I thought they were running around the forests and rolling in puddles."

"They haven't been seen in twenty-four hours. I think they've left. They should be looking after us. And one of you has told your mom that we have a camp here with not one adult or monster to take care of us. We all agreed that we wouldn't tell anybody," Koby went on dryly.

"Oh dear," Leo said. "Who told?"

Minnie blushed. "It might have been me. It was an accident, I . . ."

Minnie went quiet. Koby said: "I just wrote to our mom that we're in tents in the yard playing at camping. Maybe you should tell your parents the same."

"Playing at camping!" Halley spluttered.

"Do you have a better suggestion?" Koby snapped. He hadn't slept enough. Everything was going wrong. This was not a good time to criticize his choice of words, unless you wanted a fight.

"Everybody go home now to eat and look for your monster," Koby ordered. "I'll stay to guard the tents."

"Aren't you hungry?" Halley asked with a yawn.

"Of course I am, but you can bring me some food," Koby answered irritably.

"All right," Halley said.

"Also check that Mimi and Alice are at home. And come back soon," he continued.

Halley nodded. She had also been thinking of Mimi the night before.

"And see if there's any more fairy candy in the ceiling light for that fairy baby."

Halley nodded again. Good idea.

"And bring me some more clothes," Koby went on. "A jersey and woolly socks. And my green winter coat."

"Winter coat?" Halley repeated, puzzled.

"Yes," Koby said. "And—"

"I can't remember all that," Halley interrupted. The winter coat was the limit, actually. What kind of a servant did he think she was? A winter coat in June! Hello?

"Go get your own winter coat and woolly socks," Halley retorted.

"I'm on guard here," Koby replied crossly. "I'm trying to stay awake. And I will. Not everybody stays awake even on their watch. Like you, for example."

Halley didn't say a word but turned on her heel and left.

Koby watched her go. Well done. Now he had upset both his sisters. Really great. But the most important question was where were the monsters? Why didn't they come back? Koby could think of no sensible explanation. Did monsters go wild in a group? Maybe they were like guinea pigs, which couldn't be housed too many to a cage. Maybe they had started fighting with one another and were now lying in the forest wounded or dead, the whole lot of them. Or would they have gone on a rampage among people? And what should be done with the angry fairy-frog baby?

Frowning, Koby crawled back into the tent. Perhaps Runar would have an answer. Koby flopped down on his sleeping bag, opened the book, and began to read.

CHAPTER 24

Visible Dad

ALLEY WALKED BRISKLY ACROSS the playing field. Stupid Koby! Stupid monsters!

The soccer field was deserted, as were the yards of the buildings behind it. The whole town seemed deserted. Summer vacation! Everybody had gone to their summer cabins. Halley wished she had gone away too. What was the point in living by the sea, if you never got to go farther than the beach? If you didn't even own a rowboat, no life jackets, not one thing that was nautical and summery and fun to do? What was the point? Drat the whole summer vacation. Drat Koby and Koby's winter coat.

On the sandy lane, Halley saw three people walking toward her: a grownup and two children with lots of different bags and baskets. *There goes another family off on vacation,* Halley thought, before she realized that one of the children was wearing a blue bathrobe. Mimi! And next to Mimi was Alice, of course, and next to Alice a man who could be no other than Invisible Voice! Halley squinted with surprise. Quite a turnout, one for the books! All of a sudden, Halley was no longer seething.

Mimi waved her hand high over her head and hollered: "Halley! We've got food!"

Dad waved too, maybe. Waving one's hand is difficult if the arm is carrying a cooler and a picnic blanket. Halley waved back. Food was walking toward her. All the requested things were walking toward her. All except Koby's stupid winter coat, which Halley decided to forget about. There you go, forgotten.

The row of bushes alongside the sandy path rustled. Anybody else would have thought it was a gust of wind, but Halley knew right away: there was a monster in the bushes. The rustling progressed at the same speed as Dad, Mimi, and Alice. Would the monster come out when the bushes ended? Koby had said that monsters didn't like to move around in daylight.

Mimi, Alice, and Dad turned away from the bushes. The rustling stopped. Halley smiled to herself. The cowardly monster was staying in the bushes. Today she felt no particular sympathy toward monsters. They should have stayed where they had come from! Who needed them here? Especially if they didn't bring breakfast.

Dad stopped in front of Halley, smiling.

"Hi! We brought some picnic food," Dad said, raising the cooler.

Halley cast a critical eye on Dad, who looked at the same time familiar and like he had been away on a trip too long. He was wearing a short-sleeved shirt that was wrinkly from the suitcase and some shorts that were too new. He looked like a car salesman. His hair was combed back and his arms were pasty white. Clearly the arms of an indoor person. Dad was not a backpacker or a camper, but evidently he did know how to make picnic food.

"Not hungry?" Dad asked.

"Absolutely starving. I was just coming to get some food," Halley said.

"You don't need to now," Mimi declared happily. She didn't seem to be cross anymore either. "I've got a brilliant surprise for you. Where's Koby? And all the others? I'll tell everybody at the same time."

"Koby is at the camp, and the others went to their homes for breakfast. The monsters didn't bring any food this morning," Halley said, her eyes fixed sternly on Mimi. "Where were you all night?"

"At home investigating things," Mimi answered.

"I helped," Alice added.

"Yes, you did," Mimi confirmed.

"Let's get going now," Dad interjected good-naturedly. "You can tell us while we eat. Koby must be hungry too."

Halley smiled at Dad stiffly. The smile was a bit rusty, because she was still getting used to visible Dad. It was already clear that visible Dad was unpredictable. He might speak at any time and interrupt whenever he wanted. Who knew, he might even start giving the children good advice or tell them off.

"Koby!" Halley called. "Where are you? Come out!"

"That was quick," a voice said from a tent. Koby's head poked out of a tent doorway. "I was reading. Mimi and Alice, where on earth have you been? Oh, hi."

Koby's gaze stopped at Dad.

"You have a real proper camp here," Dad said. "Looks great. Quite a lot of tents."

"Let's put the food here," Halley said, spreading the blanket on the ground by the tent.

"Anyone else for breakfast?" Dad asked while putting the food bags on the blanket.

"No," Koby said. "They all went home to eat."

"Are you planning on camping much longer?" Dad asked.

"We might," Koby said.

Halley was unpacking the cooler. Hard-boiled eggs! Homemade cheese sandwiches! Soda in a can. Cookies and strawberries. Oranges! A perfect breakfast. Halley smiled.

Mimi looked at Koby from behind Halley.

"I forgive you," she said nobly.

"Thank you," said Koby.

"I realized that you can't help being a little bit of a chicken," Mimi went on kindly. "Maybe you'll become braver when you're older."

Halley rolled her eyes. Mimi really was one of a kind.

"Come and eat," Halley said to Koby, who nodded.

Dad watched the children. They looked different from last fall's school photos. It must have been the natural light. Children always look more alive and bigger in natural light than in photos. And they seemed to like their breakfast.

Yet Dad felt strange. It looked like time didn't move forward only where you happened to be yourself. Time passed equally quickly everywhere. Dad closed his eyes and shook his head, as if to shake out this thought that

was too strange. Then he opened his eyes and changed the subject.

"By the way, you picked a great spot for the camp. Whose idea was it?"

As Koby's and Halley's mouths were full of food, Mimi got to answer first.

"I told them to! The bathrobe said that we must move out to the yard. Then we found the spike fairy that Koby has in the jar—Koby can show you. Halley caught it in a net. Why does everybody always think that I'm making up stories? I lie the least of all! I even wanted to tell Mom that you were in a blizzard and not at home!"

"You mean you didn't tell Mom?" Dad asked, worried.

Mimi sighed and rolled her eyes. "I told you that, can't you remember?"

"What about the spike creature? May I see it?" Dad asked.

"It escaped last night," Koby said. "It had babies that came out of eggs. Then they all escaped except one. We've got it in a jar."

"Babies?" Dad repeated, disbelieving.

"Really?" Mimi yelled. "I want to see the baby!"

"It's very fierce," Koby warned.

Dad looked around. "And where are all the monsters? How many are there?"

"Thirteen," Koby said. "But I think they've run away too."

"Is that so?" Dad said.

"Yes. Even though they're supposed to take care of us. They're not supposed to leave us alone. But they're nowhere to be seen. They probably got confused when they found each other."

"What do you mean, 'confused'?" Dad asked, concerned.

"That they forgot they should be looking after us."

"And now nobody is looking after you, or at least the other children," Dad said. "I'm looking after the three of you now."

"And me," Alice remarked.

Dad looked a tiny bit worried.

"You can look after all of us at the same time," Mimi

suggested. "And the monsters are still here quite close. You just can't see them all the time."

"Do you mean that hiding dust?" Koby asked.

Mimi smiled secretively. "I have some new information," she said.

"Have you been talking to that bathrobe of yours again?" asked Halley.

Mimi nodded solemnly. "Last night, just before Dad came home."

Halley chuckled and asked Dad: "Did you get to see it?"

Dad shook his head, concerned. Because there were times when difficult things had to be done, Koby took a deep breath and said quickly: "I have seen it move. Many times, actually. Though I've never heard it speak."

Mimi gave Koby a delighted look and exclaimed: "Koby, you're not a scaredy-cat after all!"

"You're both nuts!" Halley said, laughing.

Dad cleared his throat. "We need to talk about this bathrobe thing soon," he said to Mimi. "When Mom comes home. Has she taken you to the child development clinic?"

Mimi gave Dad a puzzled look. Clinic? "I can't wait for any clinic. I'm going to tell you all right now," she said.

"Let's hear it," Koby said, and reached out to snatch a cookie. Halley took another bite of her delicious sandwich and kept shaking her head. Everything was quite crazy, but never mind. At least she wasn't hungry anymore.

"I did a few tests with Grah this morning," Mimi began. "It really can turn invisible whenever it wants. It can walk about completely invisible. Watch!"

Mimi squinted her eyes into tight slits and looked around. She jumped to her feet, took a few quick steps to the side, and blew into the air. Koby whispered to Dad: "Mimi is a little bit odd, but there's no need to worry about it," he said. "Mom says it's her age. She'll grow out of it."

Dad turned to Koby and smiled. "I know. You were a lot like her when you were younger."

Koby gave Dad a startled glance.

"Look!" Mimi yelled. "Look NOW!"

"Oh wow!" exclaimed Halley.

"What are you yelling at?" Koby asked, and turned to see. His mouth fell open. "What is that?"

In the air floated a monster's arm and a bit of its side. Really: floating in the air.

Mimi giggled and clapped her hands. "It can do that whenever it wants," she explained with glee.

"I told you so!" Halley said.

Koby screwed up his eyes. So, right in front of him, in the middle of an ordinary summer day, there was a monster. It was standing kind of hidden behind air, in its own invisibility dust.

"Very strange," Dad said, shaking his head. "I don't quite know what to think of these monsters."

Koby walked toward Mimi to get a better look at the partially visible monster.

"What if there's a strong wind?" he asked.

"I don't know. Haven't had one yet," Mimi said. "Must find out."

"Incredible," said Koby, and looked around quickly.

"Are all the other monsters somewhere around here? Can we see them by squinting?"

Mimi giggled. "No, nitwit! They'll come out when they want to."

"Do you know where they are?" Koby asked.

"The bathrobe did say something," Mimi replied mysteriously. "Want to hear?"

"I do." Koby nodded.

"First, the monsters have a home somewhere, and they want to go back there. They are really terribly homesick," she began. "But they can only get back home in some kind of a chain or line. I didn't quite understand that bit. Well, anyway. That's why they're running around the forest now. They're looking for all the monsters for the chain. One of them is missing."

Koby listened thoughtfully.

"Runar didn't write anything about chains or lines."

"Of course not," said Halley. "One monster can't form a line. Runar only knew one."

"But we have many monsters," Mimi said.

"They could be studied," Koby said. "If only they came back."

"You'll have to write a sequel to that book of Runar's," Dad said.

Koby nodded to Dad. It was possible that he understood more about things than it seemed.

"I don't understand any of this," Halley said. "What's the point of it?"

"There's probably no sense or point to it at all," Koby mused aloud.

"But guess what was the strangest thing of all?" Mimi began to chuckle. "The bathrobe said that we must look for the solution under Koby's arm! Just think, his armpit! Ha-ha!"

Alice giggled too. Dad scratched his head, confused.

Koby looked at his armpit. He was holding Runar's book there, as always.

"There's a book under my arm," Koby said, looking at Halley.

Mimi stopped laughing.

"Runar's monster book," Halley affirmed. "Koby's always carrying it around."

"And the book has several hundred pages," Koby went on. "Which one will hold the solution?"

"I don't know, but we have to look," said Halley.

"What are you talking about?" asked Mimi.

Dad smoothed Mimi's tousled hair and said: "We're saying that the solution is probably in that book."

CHAPTER 25

Visitors in the Camp

THREE LADIES APPEARED ON the edge of the playing field so suddenly that one might have thought they had dropped from the sky. The ladies were small and vaguely old, with pointed noses and very dark hair. They were dressed in similar long dresses: one red, one green, and the third gray. Their hair was twisted into a high bun on the top of their heads, and around their necks hung metal chains.

The women stood just watching for a long time. Their translucent, blank eyes studied the camp, the tents in various colors, children, one adult.

Then the ladies made a move. They approached very silently, with light steps like the wind, and not one twig or dry leaf crackled under their slippers. Nobody noticed their arrival in the camp until they were already standing in front of Dad. He had been lounging in a camping chair, reading the newspaper. A radio played music, the newspaper rustled, and Dad was humming.

"Good afternoon," said the lady in the red dress.

Startled, Dad jumped out of his chair and turned the radio down.

"Good afternoon," he said.

The ladies inclined their heads in a little bow.

"We have a camp here," Dad explained, gesturing with his hand.

"We can see that," the woman in red said. She spoke with a strange accent.

"We knew this. We came to meet you," the lady in the green dress continued.

"To meet us?" Dad repeated. "So your children are here, are they?"

"No. We are looking for the half-humans, the nanny monsters," the lady in gray replied.

"Oh, the monsters," Dad began. "Are they yours? I do have a few questions—"

"We do not see them here," gray dress interrupted coolly. "Where are they?"

Koby sat up on his blanket in front of the tent. He had been reading Runar's book when the ladies came but quickly covered it up. For some reason, he didn't want these visitors to see his book.

"They've run away," Koby answered.

"Run away," the woman in the green dress repeated. "Could you tell us when and how?"

"Yesterday morning they made us breakfast, but we haven't seen them since," Koby said. "I think they've run away. They do run very fast."

"But there is one still here," Dad said to Koby. "That one of ours, the one with a name. Where is it?"

Koby, Halley, and Mimi kept their eyes on the ground. Apparently, Dad could still be perfectly stupid. Anybody with any sense could see that there was no way they'd give Grah up to these women.

"Please, go get the half-human. We'll take it with us," said the woman in the gray.

"Mimi, where is it?" Dad asked helpfully.

"Sorry, but it ran off too," Mimi replied sadly. She gave a warning look to Alice, who kept looking in the direction where Grah had been painting with watercolors a moment ago. The spot was empty, the paints and brushes lying on the ground.

"Oh, really?" Dad said, giving Mimi a puzzled look. The three peculiar women also turned their translucent eyes to Mimi. Mimi's skin went goose pimply. Their gazes went right through to her bones. Mimi returned the look calmly. Dad frowned and eyed the women.

"Excuse me, but who are you, exactly?" Dad asked. "Are you the monsters' owners? Did you send them?"

The women turned toward Dad, and Mimi sighed with relief.

"We received notice that the monsters had left the places to which they were sent. We came to find them. They have failed to obey orders and will be sent for further training."

"Further training, is it. Where did you get the monsters?" Dad asked. "And how do you train them?"

"We have the best trainers," the woman in red replied.

"Can the monsters go to that school whenever they want to?" Koby asked.

The ladies gave a brief, dry laugh all at the same time. Obviously, they had thought Koby's question amusing. Koby received no other reply.

"Well, everybody should be allowed to decide for themselves if they want to go to school or stay at home!" Mimi declared, riled up. "Just think if you were forced to—"

"Mimi," Dad interrupted. "Could you fetch me a fork from that last tent, please?"

"Bah," Mimi huffed, but went because she wasn't stupid.

"It was all our fault that they ran off," Koby said. "We

took them to the forest and let them loose. We told them to go and eat."

"You did not follow the instructions," said the one in gray.

"They were hungry," Koby replied.

"And so you decided to take them out to eat?" the one in green asked.

Koby nodded uncertainly. He didn't want to reveal Runar's book.

The women studied each other slowly, as if reading secret messages on each other's faces. The one in red spoke: "So, you are the . . . father?"

"Yes, I am," Dad answered. "Of these two here." Dad pointed at Halley and Koby. "And the one who went to get a fork. The rest are other people's children."

Dad pointed around the camp vaguely.

The women nodded and looked at one another.

Halley looked at Koby and giggled. Koby grinned. These women were not quite normal.

The woman in gray turned to Koby, who quickly wiped the grin off his face. He hoped the woman hadn't seen it.

"Are you looking after all these children?" red dress asked Dad.

Dad nodded hesitantly. The women looked at one another again. Then all three suddenly smiled at the same time. They had very white, tiny, pointed teeth.

"Are these children safe in the camp?"

"Of course," Dad said, alarmed.

"Excellent," the one in red said.

"May we ask where that sound is coming from?" asked the woman in green.

"What sound?" Dad was confused. There was no sound.

"Something is knocking on glass," the woman said. "The sound is coming from there."

The woman turned toward Koby's tent. Koby glanced at Halley. The baby mosquito-fairy. How could the woman hear such a tiny sound? They had given the creature the last fairy candy they had found, which had evidently given it strength and made it even angrier than before. Now the mosquito-fairy baby was attacking the jar walls nonstop. The children had no idea how they could ever feed it again, because nobody dared to open the lid.

"It's that mosquito-fairy," Dad said, and set off toward the tent. "In fact, you could take a look at it. Perhaps you know what it is."

Halley ground her teeth together. Dad was such an utter blabbermouth.

Dad returned with the jar and handed it to the woman in red. She raised the glass cookie jar up to her translucent eyes.

"Where did you get this?" she asked.

"It hatched out of an egg last night," Halley said. "Its mother and siblings escaped."

"So they're missing too," the woman said. "How many were there?"

"Maybe six," Koby guessed. "What are they?"

"They are beach spikes, also known as botherfairies. They should not be here. It is best we take it with us," the woman in gray said. "They are aggressive as juveniles."

Koby nodded. He was happy to part with the botherfairy.

"When the monsters return, please inform us without delay," said the one in green, and handed a card to Dad. "Here is my calling card."

Dad took it as if it were normal to receive calling cards.

"Thank you, we certainly will," Dad replied in a reliable dad voice.

"Good," said the woman in the red dress. "Good evening to you."

The women bowed their goodbyes and stepped off toward the forest behind the tents. Dad and the children stared after them. The women moved in an oddly even way. Almost as if the grass were propelling them forward.

"What a strange visit," Dad said, and looked at the card. "Wonder whose evil fairy godmothers they were. Let's see."

The card was blank. Dad scrunched it up and put it in

his pocket. "It takes all kinds. Didn't seem quite normal. Scary ladies. Halley, can you turn the radio up, please? The news is on."

The newscaster's soothing voice filled the air. Dad flopped back into his camping chair.

". . . particularly the forests in the eastern part of the town have suffered repeated vandalism and damage. In many places, young trees less than six feet in height have been torn off at their roots, and protected blue anemones and various mosses and lichens have been trampled and dug up. The flowers in the rhododendron park on East Beach have been pulled off, piled up in a heap, and apparently trampled or flattened with some large object. No reason has been found for the vandalism. Moreover, it is clear that these are the actions of a large band of vandals, maybe even several separate groups, as many of the sites are a long way apart . . ."

"Did you hear that, Halley?" Koby said.

"Course I did," Halley answered.

Obviously the monsters were still somewhere nearby. A broad grin spread across Koby's face. Dad noticed it and asked: "Children. Do tell me: Why do you want the monsters to come back?"

"We don't want them back," Koby answered. "We want to get them back to their own homes. So that they don't have to lurk around the forest or live in people's hall closets. And so those witches don't get to train them any-more."

Dad nodded thoughtfully. It was all beginning to make sense.

"So what we actually have here is a monsters' libera-tion camp," Dad said.

Halley and Koby nodded. Exactly.

Meanwhile, the three women walked past the last tent and stopped at the forest's edge. Mimi happened to be stand-ing behind the last tent, and she quickly crouched down. She could hear them speak in an unknown language. One of them was shaking a big, round object in her hands, but what was it? It was hard to see.

At last the women seemed to reach agreement. The one in green stopped shaking the object, and Mimi finally saw what it was: the mosquito-fairy's jar. Why did they have it? But even stranger things were coming. The woman unscrewed the lid, pushed her narrow hand into the cookie jar, and brought out the mosquito-fairy, hanging by one leg. The angry spike fairy wriggled and shrieked shrilly, but the women scarcely glanced at it, just went on talking. Suddenly the woman in green threw the mosquito into her mouth and swallowed it. Mimi's jaw dropped.

The women then quickly turned toward the forest and vanished into it like mist.

CHAPTER 26

The Map

KOBY LAY IN THE hammock reading Runar's book. He was becoming quite certain of one thing: the book didn't contain a single word about monster packs and their behavior. Not a word about training monsters and having them work as nannies. Nothing on botherfairies or spine-chilling fairy godmothers, witches, or whatever they were. But worst of all was that Runar's book contained not a thing about monster chains or their returning home. Runar had had no idea about them. Everything was left for future researchers — in other words, for Koby — to find out.

Koby stopped reading and watched the ragged clouds drifting across the blue sky. It was a sunny day, there was a slight wind, and almost everybody had gone to the beach. The camp was silent apart from the slight flapping of Grah's watercolor paintings hanging on clotheslines. Grah no longer made breakfast or hid during the day. Ever since Dad had arrived at the camp, all Grah had done was paint. Mimi and Alice would sit next to it like two small guard dogs. As if Grah needed anyone to protect it.

Koby closed his eyes and thought for the hundredth, maybe thousandth, time: *Can the bathrobe be trusted? Does a sensible human being rely on the advice of a bathrobe? If the bathrobe said that the solution was to be found in the book, could one be sure? And what if it wasn't?*

Koby opened his eyes and sighed. He carried on reading. What else could a sensible human do?

Meanwhile, at the edge of the forest, Grah's latest painting was finished. It bore an uncanny resemblance to all the others, and they were not much to write home about. Grah's watercolor pictures were all waterlogged messes with dark colors slapped all over the paper. Alice yawned; Mimi sighed. The guard dogs were very bored.

Grah got up clumsily. It stepped to the clothesline and tenderly hung yet another painting up to dry.

"Maybe it's not allowed to paint in its own home," Alice whispered to Mimi, who was rolling her eyes up to the sky. Grah had painted enough!

"Grah, let's do something else for a change," Mimi suggested.

Grah did not answer. It was fully immersed in the job at hand. Having hung up the picture, it moved over to the next clothesline, dust flying from its coat.

The papers painted in the morning swayed in the wind, dry, but just as ugly as before. Grah removed the clothespins and gently gathered the papers in its arms.

Mimi and Alice exchanged looks. This was something new. Up to now, Grah had only painted and hung, over and over again. This was the first time it had taken anything off the line. The monster pattered back to the grass with its pile of paper, plopped down, and started to examine its paintings in detail. Some of them it put down, adding a stone so they wouldn't blow away.

"What is it doing?" Alice asked.

"I haven't a clue," Mimi replied. "Let's go and take a look."

"Can I help?" Mimi asked. Grah's wild yellow eyes turned to Mimi. The creature let out a hollow growl. Mimi laughed and sat down on the ground next to Grah.

"OK, what do we do?" she asked.

A couple of hours later, the others all returned from the beach.

"Today's cooks are Oscar, Minnie, Alba, Jenna, and Leo," Dad called out. "Will you go to Leo's to make the stew? Good. And clearing up after the meal, Elijah, Luke, Anna, Jemima, and . . ."

Dad saw that Koby had fallen asleep in the hammock under his book. He would let him sleep, poor lad.

". . . and Halley," Dad went on. "Everybody else on free time until dinner."

The upshot of the visit by the three strange ladies was that Dad had realized that he was the only responsible adult in the camp — in other words, the camp leader. Did he want to be the camp leader? That question hadn't been put to him, since there were no other adult leaders available. Dad had no choice but to rise to the occasion and fill the leader's boots thrust upon him.

It was the fourth camp day, and Dad had already improved significantly. He remembered the children's names. He did not forget mealtimes, or at least the fact that they had to eat several times a day. He realized that the jobs had to be shared and that the children could not be allowed to go swimming alone. He was feeling proud of himself. He looked around the camp for Mimi and Alice. They weren't still sitting with the monster behind the tents? Dad walked over to the forest edge and heard Mimi's voice.

"Here? No? Where, then?" Mimi was asking.

Dad stopped behind the two girls and the monster.

"What are you up to?" he asked.

"We think Grah is making a jigsaw puzzle, although it probably doesn't form a picture. Look for yourself!" Mimi waved her hand.

Dad looked. He watched his youngest daughter place painted pieces on the grass according to the monster's directions. He looked at the strange picture made up by the smaller paintings, already covering several square yards. Everything looked like it was happening as if there was some sense and logic behind it.

"How do you actually understand Grah?" Dad asked.

"Just normally," Mimi said, and gave Dad a surprised look. "In the same way as one understands anybody. Just like I understand you."

"Oh," said Dad, frowning. "Are you saying it can talk?"

"In a way," Mimi said. "Not in words, more with its eyes and fingers."

"Eyes and fingers, is it," Dad repeated. "Do I talk with my eyes and fingers, then?"

Mimi laughed. Dad was just like Halley. Immediately got bogged down in thinking of himself. Even if others were talking about something completely different! It seemed a bit childish, even though Dad was a grownup, beard and all.

"No, now you mostly talk quite normally. You used to talk mainly on the phone," Mimi said with a grin.

The girls and Grah continued putting the jigsaw together.

"Which one next?" Mimi asked.

With its thick fingers, Grah clumsily flipped through the pile of paintings. When it found the correct picture, Grah picked it up between its fingers and set it in its place gently, as if it were a baby bird.

"Alice, stones, please," Mimi asked. Alice skipped to the paper and put stones around the edges to weight them down. Dad noticed that there were four small stones holding down every picture.

"You are such clever children," Dad said.

"Of course," Mimi said. "Which picture comes next?"

Grah continued flipping through the paintings.

"By the way, that looks a bit like a map when you look at it from a distance," Dad said, pointing at it. "Take a look. That is just like this field from above. There is the forest and here the field. Those red blobs at the edge of the field must be the tents. Do you see? There are those trees, one of them much bigger than the others. Don't you think?"

Mimi stood up and looked. Maybe. It was possible.

"Grah, is this a map? Have you drawn a map for us?"

Grah grunted.

"What did that mean?" Dad asked.

"It meant, 'perhaps,' " Mimi said.

"Perhaps? You don't understand it after all?" Dad asked.

"I told you, I understand it in the same way as everybody else. It means: roughly speaking."

Dad studied the picture further. The messy watercolor paintings were not just messes anymore. Looking at them from farther away, they formed figures and clear color areas. Dad shook his head, puzzled.

Grah had painted a large map.

"Look. There's the sea. Here's the marina. Here's the path to it. Do you see?" Dad explained to Mimi and Alice.

The girls agreed.

"What are those?" Dad asked, pointing at little light spots near the shore on the water.

"Stars?" Alice suggested.

"Stars in summer?" Dad asked.

Grah grunted. Awkwardly, it got to its feet and scratched its right arm, as if looking for something in its fur. A small dust cloud puffed up, lumps of earth dropped to the ground, and Mimi sneezed, but Grah found what it was looking for. It handed a tiny gray bundle to Mimi with a grunt.

"What's this?" Mimi asked, and started opening it. "Some piece of paper."

Mimi carefully smoothed out the paper. It was gray and torn, but she recognized it instantly.

"The spike fairy's candy wrapper!" Mimi exclaimed. "Why did you give it to me?"

Grah picked up the wrapper, bent over the map, and put the paper on it over the light spots.

"Are the spike fairies down there on the beach?" Mimi asked.

Grah grunted.

"Do you see now, this is how I understand it," Mimi said to Dad, who nodded. Mimi turned back to Grah.

"Do you know where the other monsters are?"

Grah waved its hand over the map. It did not stop but covered all parts of it.

"Scattered all over the place," Mimi interpreted. "Will you help us find them?"

Suddenly Grah bent down and slapped the map hard

with its hand. Its palm hit a spot on the map where there was a little rocky crag on the edge of the forest.

Dad jumped. Alice let out a little frightened squeak.

"Oops," said Mimi. "Are you cross?"

Grah kneeled down, smoothing a rip that it had made, murring quietly.

"What is the matter with it?" Dad asked.

"Is it upset because the paper is torn?" Alice said.

"No, it's missing something," Mimi said in a low voice. "Grah, is your home on the map?"

Grah lifted its yellow eyes and stopped stroking the map. The big, dark hand rested over the rip.

"Is it there?" Mimi asked. "Where you hit it?"

Grah grunted. Mimi's cheeks were pink with excitement as she turned to Dad and said: "We've got to get Koby and Halley here. Quickly. Now we know where the monsters' home is."

Mimi turned to Grah and said, her voice trembling with enthusiasm: "Grah, you darling monster. Don't worry about anything. We will take you home."

CHAPTER 27

The Forest at Night

THERE," HALLEY SAID QUICKLY, pointing up. "Did you see?"

"No," Minnie said, peering at the sky.

"Where?" Dad asked.

Koby kept his eyes in the direction Halley pointed, but the night sky over the marina was empty. Not a single luminous botherfairy in sight.

"It'll be back soon," Halley mumbled, eyes skyward.

"Was it on its own?" Koby asked.

"Might have been—I didn't see it clearly," Halley said. "It was visible for such a short time."

"We'll wait," Dad said.

The dark bushes at the forest edge were whispering, the boats clanked eerily on their moorings, and all around there were little rustlings, whistlings, poppings. It felt like there was something inexplicable, almost ominous, adrift in the summer night. Almost as if the children and Dad were sitting under a bush expecting something evil and dangerous, even though they only wanted to see the botherfairies. Preferably from afar, but still.

"Why are they called botherfairies? I wonder if they bother people as well as monsters?" Koby was thinking aloud, but nobody replied.

"And where is that knocking coming from?" Halley asked nervously. "Just like someone beating flagpoles with a coat hanger."

"It's coming from the sailboats," Oscar said. "The halyards have been left too slack. The wind knocks them against the aluminum masts. They should be tightened up more. Dad's always telling the others."

Halley looked at Oscar, surprised.

"You go sailing, then? Vacation cabin on an island and so on?"

"Well, we have a boat. No cabin," Oscar said.

"Wow," said Halley. "I'll come sailing with you sometime."

Oscar shrugged. "OK by me."

"Hey, look, over there," Minnie whispered suddenly. "There, do you see?"

Koby whistled.

"There are a lot more than six," he said.

"Well, I say," Dad whispered. "Are you sure they're not fireflies?"

"Fireflies are smaller," said Koby.

"There's at least twenty of them," Minnie reckoned.

"More," Koby said. "Forty or fifty."

"Maybe they lay a lot of eggs quickly," Halley said. "Or else someone has left the door open."

"What door?" Minnie asked.

"The door through which monsters and fairies and fairy godmothers come," Halley said, smiling.

"Ha-ha, very funny." Dad chuckled.

"Whatever are they doing now?" Minnie asked a moment later.

The flashing creatures had been flying in circles around the sailboat masts, but now they formed a line like a long snake. The snake of light flew a few quick, elegant loops in the air, and then . . . yikes! It shot forward like an arrow straight toward the spot where Halley, Koby, Minnie, Oscar, and Dad were crouching.

"They're attacking!" Minnie whispered, alarmed.

"Down, everybody!" Dad commanded, and flopped on his belly. "Cover your eyes!"

"But why . . . ?" Koby managed to say, before Dad yanked him to the ground. Halley fell on her back next to Koby, but she couldn't close her eyes. She couldn't look away from the flying streak of light, which came closer, closer, closer and . . .

"They flew over us!" Halley cried, surprised.

"What?" Oscar asked in a muffled voice from underneath Koby.

"They weren't heading for us," Halley replied, and sat up. "They flew straight into the forest."

"What are they doing there?" Oscar asked.

"Looking for food, perhaps. Or the monsters," Halley suggested.

"Let's go back to the camp," Oscar asked.

Dad nodded in agreement. "Good idea. We've seen what we came to see. In any case, all the others are sure to be asleep by now."

Dad was wrong. Not everybody was asleep. How could Mimi sleep when she had just found out where the monsters' home might be? How could anybody with any sense believe that Mimi could wait until tomorrow, even though the camp leader might think it best? Of course, Mimi wanted to see the monsters' house door immediately. And if Mimi was awake, so was Alice. And Grah . . . well, its sleeping was something of a mystery anyway.

While the camp leader crouched under a bush in the marina watching the night sky, three shadows bent low sneaked out of the camp. One of the shadows was very big and bulky; two were very small and quick. Ever deeper into the forest and ever farther from the camp they crept, until the biggest of them unexpectedly bent down and picked up the two small ones, one under each arm. There was sneezing and giggling. Mimi, Alice, and Grah were on their way to see Grah's home, and they didn't even need Grah's big map—the monster knew the way.

"Alice, you should close your eyes now," Mimi advised.

"Why?" Alice kept sneezing.

"You'll find out soon!" Mimi said, and sneezed.

Grah headed down the forest path with the girls under its arms, picking up speed with every step. The ground boomed, tree branches swiped at them, dry twigs snapped, and the scenery whizzed by as if they were on a merry-go-round. Mimi laughed aloud, but Alice clung to Grah's arm and hid her face against the monster's shoulder. Not everybody likes the craziest rides in the amusement park.

Gradually, they slowed down. They had reached a little clearing in the forest, with a tall greenish-brown rock rising on one side like a wall. The rock wall was at least ten feet high, and on top of it stood an oddly shaped mound of stones.

An old pine tree had fallen next to the rock, and its huge root ball rose out of the earth, as if opening a doorway deep into it.

Grah set the girls down. It was murring a low, nervous hum and stepped hesitantly toward the rock wall, closer and closer, until its face was almost touching the rock. It remained standing there as if waiting for something.

"I wonder if it thinks it has one of those automatic

sliding doors like at the supermarket," Alice whispered to Mimi.

"I don't think so, but there is something special about that rock," Mimi whispered.

"I wonder if the door of its home has moved," Alice pondered aloud, but Mimi shook her head.

"Doors don't move," she said, and crept up to Grah. Mimi slipped her little hand into the monster's big warm one and gave it an encouraging squeeze.

"Is this where the door should be? Except that we can't see it?" Mimi asked quietly.

Grah said nothing, of course. Its strange glowing eyes glanced at Mimi's worried almond eyes. It looked sad.

"Oh, you darling monster," Mimi whispered, and stroked its thick arm. "It'll be OK. Alice and I will help you. You'll get home. We'll find that door."

"Mimi," Alice squealed suddenly in a very small and scared voice. "Look."

Mimi turned to Alice, whose eyes, round with fright, were fixed on the top of the rock behind Mimi. Mimi turned to follow Alice's gaze. Grah started to make a low murring sound.

High up on the rock stood a strange gray monster. It looked like a huge, scary shadow against the night sky. The creature's glowing eyes shone yellow and wild, as it stared down into the clearing. The monster looked older, stronger, and wilder than Grah or any of the monsters Mimi had seen.

One of its ears hung down as if it was partly torn. Mimi was certain she had not seen the monster before, but why did it feel somehow familiar? That ear and the gray coat . . . Suddenly she remembered.

"That's the monster in Runar's book," Mimi whispered, and turned to Grah. "You know it, don't you?"

Grah let out a long, moaning roar, which echoed throughout the silent forest. Alice covered her ears with her hands. When the forest was quiet again, Runar's monster had gone.

CHAPTER 28

The Missing Page

KOBY SAT IN DAD's camping chair, listening to the news on the radio. The newscaster's neutral voice read:

". . . damage has been found almost daily in the forests and waterside areas of the east side of the town. Up to now, the vandalism has been targeted at nature, and cars, boats, and other valuable private property have been left untouched. However, the damage to forest and parkland areas has been considerable. Security has been tightened, and the police say that many volunteers have also come forward to help protect the areas. The problem is the large size of the affected area. The police also say that it is imperative to eliminate the possibility that the cause could be some animal, as scientists specializing in large wild animals say that certain features of the detruction may also indicate a fairly large herd or pack of animals . . ."

Koby shook his head. Sooner or later someone was going to see the monsters, if they continued running around the forests like this. If only they had the sense to return to the children they were supposed to be taking care of! Koby had given a lot of thought as to why they didn't and believed that he understood now. The monsters must have thought that the children would send them back to the three witches' monster school! They didn't know that everybody in the camp, even Halley, wanted to help the monsters to get back to their home, away from the witches and the hall closets. The only thing missing from the rescue plan was the monsters. They had Grah's map. And they still had Grah, though it had been behaving very strangely since it had finished its painting and mostly just sat morosely under the weeping willows.

The news ended, the weather forecast began, and Koby clicked the radio off. He had heard all he wanted to hear.

Silence and perfect peace for reading descended on the camp. The others were on the beach, shopping, wherever. Koby had wanted to stay as camp guard, as it allowed him to read without interruptions. He got out of the camping chair and set off toward his tent to get Runar's book.

The tent door hung half open. Koby stopped. He was sure he had zipped it up properly in the morning. He always zipped it up properly. Oscar had gone to the beach ages ago. Had someone gone into his tent?

Koby's eyes swept along the row of tents, the forest edge, and the big playing field. He checked out the clotheslines, now hung with only beach towels. All was quiet, peaceful, and quite ordinary. His heart pounding, Koby undid the zipper fully and peeked inside. Everything looked the same as that morning: sleeping bags, backpacks, pillows. But the uneasy feeling was still there.

Runar's book lay on the floor of the tent. Koby picked it up and squeezed it under his arm. He went back to Dad's camping chair and opened the book. He instantly felt better. Books calmed Koby down. His eyes automatically started to read; everything became easy and understandable. Koby browsed through the pages, looking for something he hadn't read yet. His gaze stopped at "Chapter 12: Some Unusual Observations."

Koby knew this chapter. It was long and confusing. He had read bits here and there, but never all of it. It was not one of the most interesting chapters in the book, rather just a list or record of facts without any answers. But he didn't need anything interesting right now. He needed something calming.

Koby took one more look around, enjoying the silence. He began to read.

This chapter was written with the researchers of future years in mind, who will have better daily opportunities of immersing themselves in the lives of monsters than I have. First of all, I must acknowledge the shortcomings of this attempt at a chapter, as there are plenty. These facts I am unable to explain or link to a larger whole. I have merely observed them and recorded them. Thus, this chapter is rather like an archive shelf, onto which I throw my unfinished information. I record many of my individual little observations, which my scientist's instinct tells me definitely mean something, although their significance is not yet known to me.

On many occasions, I have observed various things, decided that they may be important in one way or another, even though their relevance . . .

Yaaaawn! Runar was apt to go on and on forever before he got to the point. Koby scanned the next page. Notes about the way the monster seemed to turn up unnoticed, then a little bit about caring for its coat, then about some disease affecting its nails, then about things that seemed to attract the monster, behavior during full moon . . . Just a minute. Things that attracted the monster? Perhaps things that could tempt escaped monsters back to the camp? Koby started reading.

As I mentioned above, the reflection of a mirror attracts the monster. So does the smell of carrot, even though it is not interested in eating carrots. A certain kind of slow guitar music always receives its undivided attention. On many occasions, a bucket of water was also sufficient to tempt it, often merely the gentle splashing of water with one's hand . . .

Gentle splashing of water! A pack of monsters that had run away into the forest would definitely not be enticed back by splashing water or a bag of carrots. These instructions were for close tempting, at short distances, and did not fit the situation at hand. Koby scanned the text further.

. . . like many other living things. There is something about the full moon that affects us deeply. In the same way, on that night the monster was ready to jump out of its skin and was itching to get out of the house. At first, I misinterpreted it as a desire to go hunting, but the more I learned about the monster's true character, the more clearly I understood that this was about something else. And before long, with the help of my calendar notes, I realized that this unusual behavior was linked to the full moon.

Finally, after getting up courage, I decided to conduct an experiment. On a night with the full moon, I put a chain around the monster's neck. We went out together. The monster was skittish, like a cow put out to pasture for the first time in spring. So we half ran, half walked, sometimes stumbled through the forest, to a small rock formation nearby. On the left-hand side of the rock there is a strange cairn of stones shaped like a bottle, higher than a man, which is why the rock was called Bottle Rock . . .

"Bottle Rock," Koby repeated, surprised. How had he managed to miss this before? It was the same place Grah had marked on the map as its home, and where Mimi claimed to have seen Runar's monster. Had Runar lived around here, someplace nearby? Koby carried on reading.

Bottle Rock was indeed the destination of the monster's pilgrimage. Having made it there, that big black creature stopped only when it had gotten as close to the rock as it was possible to get: it remained standing in front of the rock with its face almost touching the wall. Every so often, it looked at the moon, as if waiting for something, then turned to the rock again. Standing in front of the rock, the monster appeared to be sad rather than happy. The whole night was spent here. Nothing else happened. After the first night, I let the monster run to the rock at every full moon, which it always did with great enthusiasm. I never found the reason for this urge. I leave this matter to the future generations, future researchers.

Koby lifted his eyes from the book. Mimi's story of Grah at Bottle Rock had been exactly like this, with the exception of the full moon. But why did Runar's monster only want to go to the rock during the full moon? Was that the only time the door opened to its home? Would all the monsters go to Bottle Rock at the full moon? Koby's forehead creased with thinking. When was the next full moon?

Koby closed the book and, deep in thought, stroked its old, soft spine. Suddenly his finger touched a little scrap of paper poking out of the pages toward the end. What was it? The page wasn't torn, was it?

Koby opened the book at the ragged page. His heart missed a beat. The page was not torn—something much worse had happened: a whole page had been ripped out. Koby was so shocked that he almost shook. Someone had gone into his tent, taken the book, and torn a page out of it. Who, why, when? What was on the stolen page?

Koby studied the place where the page was ripped out. It wasn't hard to work out which page was missing: the picture of Runar's monster. The very page that had made Grah cry.

CHAPTER 29

Full Moon

F ULL MOON," DAD SAID, gazing at the light summer sky, preoccupied. "When is it? Anybody know?"

"My dad would know," said Oscar.

"Show-off," Halley muttered. Fancy having to defend your dad, who doesn't know when it's a full moon.

"All grownups generally know such things," Minnie muttered, looking at her toes.

"I don't know," Dad said, surprised. "How is one supposed to know that?"

"One could look it up in a calendar," said Oscar.

"Well, let's look. Who has a calendar on them?" Dad asked, looking at the children standing around him.

Silence. Nobody had a calendar.

"I'll go to the library on my bike and look it up," said

Koby. He glanced at his watch. "Exactly half an hour before the library closes. Watch the book."

Dad and Halley nodded. They were all bothered by the thought that someone had been lurking around their camp while they were away. Someone who knew about the book and monsters. Did they know about anything else?

"You did reply to Mom, didn't you?" Dad checked before Koby set off.

"Yes, I did."

"And what did Mom say?" Dad asked.

"That you must answer her messages."

Dad laughed.

"OK. Lucky the phone battery is charged up now. Let's go and see what Mom has to say," he said to Mimi and Alice, grabbing the giggling girls under each arm. "And then we'll pop home and wash that bathrobe of Mimi's. It looks more gray than blue these days. It's probably too dirty to even talk."

They had come a long way since the days of Invisible Voice, Halley thought, watching them go.

Koby jogged to their yard and got his bike. He had no time to lose. He jumped into the saddle and started pedaling. Without a sideways glance, he shot though the parking lot, swung down a steep little hill, and was just whizzing past Café Rio when something made him brake as hard as he could. Out of the corner of his eye, he had seen something familiar. Koby let the bike drop to the ground and ran up to the café window.

An advertisement from the evening paper had been taped to the window. In the grainy, poor-quality photo from the front page, a great grayish monster stared back at him. It had obviously just been eating a moldy pile of leaves or dried twigs. It had been caught in the act, and in the picture it had just turned its furious face toward the photographer.

His heart thumping, Koby dug about in his pockets, but he had no money. The café owner appeared at the door and yelled at him:

"Hey, pick up your bike! You can't leave it in the middle of the road!"

"Excuse me, but could I have a look at that paper?" Koby asked, out of breath.

The man eyed Koby.

"There are no papers left. Sold them all. People are scared, and that sells. They say that picture was taken somewhere not far away, one or two miles from here."

"Did they catch them?" Koby asked fearfully.

The café owner chuckled. "Don't be too frightened, kiddo. There was just the one animal. The police will catch it tomorrow—they'll mount a major search operation! They're just wondering which zoo it's escaped from. And what the creature actually is."

Koby stared at the photo. The café man didn't understand that Koby was afraid not for himself, but for the monster. For all the monsters. Time was running out.

"When is the full moon?" he asked abruptly.

"Full moon, eh?" the café owner echoed, taken aback. "It's tonight. Just noticed on my calendar."

"Are you sure?" Koby asked, white as a sheet.

The man smiled.

"Quite sure. What do you need to know that for?"

"Just interested," Koby replied hurriedly. "Got to go. Thanks!"

The man was shaking his head as Koby jumped on his bike and set off back to camp as speedily as he could. Throwing his bike down as he sprinted toward the tents, he realized that there were visitors. He stopped and hid behind a bush. These visitors he did not want to meet. The three witches were back.

Koby peered through the branches and watched. Dad seemed to be heatedly gesturing toward the tents. He was pointing at the kids, who were standing in a group around him. The women waited. Dad dropped his hands and fell silent. His posture showed defeat. The conversation continued, but Koby couldn't hear what was being said. In the end the women bowed goodbye and headed toward the forest behind the tents, their skirts sweeping the ground. Koby waited a moment, then picked up his bike and pushed it into camp. Dad saw him and raised his hand in a subdued greeting.

"What happened?" Koby asked.

"I think our camp might be over," Dad said, smiling sadly.

"What do you mean?" Koby said.

"The monsters have not been found, and your mother's trip in Lapland is being cut short. Everybody is coming home tomorrow. That's what those women said."

"So Mom is coming home?" Koby asked.

"Well, of course she is! She won't be staying in Lapland on her own," Halley snapped irritably.

"Why can't you carry on looking after all of us?" Koby asked Dad.

Dad shrugged.

The children looked miserable. They had been having a great time, and now this. This was the first summer vacation when it hadn't been deadly boring at home or they hadn't been forced to attend some weird class on growing vegetables in containers.

"When will Mom be home?" Koby asked.

"They'll all be home in the morning," Dad said.

"Our last night in the tents," Minnie said quietly.

"It could be a good thing too," Dad said.

"How could it?" Minnie asked. "We haven't even found the monsters."

"Not yet, but someone has seen them," Koby said. "There was a photo of one on the front page of the evening paper. There'll be a big search operation here tomorrow."

"No!" yelled Mimi. "No, no, no!"

"It's crazy. Parents let monsters take care of their kids, but they won't let you," Halley raged to Dad. "Really sensible."

Dad smiled lamely.

"So where are they supposedly putting the monsters if they catch them?" Mimi asked crossly. "Grah at least can live in our hall closet for as long as it wants. Never mind what Mom says!" Then she let out a sob.

"But tonight is a full moon," Koby pointed out.

"Really?" Halley piped up.

Mimi stopped sobbing and looked at Koby. In fact, everybody was looking at Koby.

"Really," Koby said.

"Quite sure?" Mimi asked.

"Quite sure," Koby said. "The camp is over, but perhaps we can still get the monsters back to their home."

Following a moment of stunned silence, Dad said: "OK. We'll have something to eat and take a little nap so that we can stay awake until the moon comes up."

Mimi and Alice leapt up and cheered.

CHAPTER 30

Door to Home

THE NIGHT WAS CLOUDY and darker than usual. The moon was out of sight, hiding behind the raggedy clouds drifting across the sky. Tonight, nobody had stayed in the camp to sleep. The entire camp was trekking in a silent, nervous line along a forest path that almost disappeared under vegetation.

Grah had been walking at the head of the line, but then it had suddenly vanished. All evening it had been jumpy and growly, continually peering in different directions, listening for sounds coming from the forest and beach.

"Where did Grah go?" asked Mimi, worried.

"It's probably running around the forest like the others," Koby said.

"What if it can't find its way to the rock? Or if it's

late?" Mimi went on, miserably pushing her hands into her bathrobe pockets.

"Mimi, of course it can. Grah drew the map," Halley pointed out dryly.

The path wound close to the marina. The boats rocked in the dark water; the masts clanged. There was no sign of the botherfairies.

"I wonder what happens to those spike fairies when the monsters leave?" Mimi asked. "What will they eat then?"

"Maybe they follow the monsters. They followed them here," Koby replied patiently.

"Could we follow the monsters too?" Mimi asked quietly.

"Are you quite mad?" Halley huffed.

"It's not easy to get to the monsters' home," Koby said. "If that monster you saw really was Runar's monster, it's been looking for its home for eighty years. And it's still here."

"Maybe it just doesn't want to go home. It's had much more fun here," Halley said. "Maybe their home is a really horrid place. They have to go to the three witches' school, and all kinds of spiky creatures attack them all the time."

"Grah seems to want to go back," Koby pointed out. "And according to Runar, the first monster did too."

Mimi sighed and stroked her bathrobe. She missed their conversations. She missed its advice. When would it talk again?

"So not fair that all the monsters must go home together or nobody can go," Mimi said. "What if one of them doesn't feel like going? Or it's sick or something?"

"Life is unfair," Halley muttered.

"That chain thing is just like kindergarten outings, when everybody must hold on to a rope. If one is lost, everybody must stop and look for them, or you can't go on," Mimi continued.

"Perhaps Runar's monster was part of a different chain," Halley said in a prickly tone. "How do we even know if Runar's monster is in any way connected to the others?"

Mimi sighed.

"Nitwit! Use your brain. Which monster was the very first?" she insisted.

"Mimi could be right," Koby said. "First came Runar's monster and then the others. After all, there must be some reason why they all want to go to the same place at the time of a full moon."

"If they even do want to," Halley said.

"Halley, stop it. We'll soon see," Koby said.

They trekked on in silence. The clouds sailed in the sky; the night shadows flitted on the ground. The path became ever narrower. The ghostly forest seemed to close up around them, to hug them out of sight. What else was it hiding? Somewhere behind the dense branches and night clouds was the full moon.

At last they came to the foot of the rock. The vertical wall rose in front of them, mossy and dark. In the half-light, the roots of the fallen tree looked like a giant sleeping bear. The bottle-shaped pile of stones was a dark shadow against the sky.

"We have arrived," Dad said.

"What do we do now?" asked Oscar. "There's nobody here."

"We'll sit down and wait," replied Koby.

They sat. It sounded like the forest was breathing. It hissed, whooshed, and rustled and was never silent for a moment.

"There's a wind getting up," Dad said. "That's good. We might see the moon soon, if the wind blows the clouds away."

They sat silently again. Nobody felt like talking. But Dad was right. Gradually, the sky cleared and the moon came out, ghostly, huge, and round. It cast a weak light over the Bottle Rock clearing and made Halley shudder. Mimi and Alice pressed themselves against her. In fact, all of them huddled against one another.

"Monster mosquitoes," Mimi whispered.

"Where?" said Alice.

Halley pointed toward the sky.

High up in the sky, they saw a cloud formed by tiny dots of light. The cloud was moving away from Bottle Rock.

"Good thing they're moving away, so that the monsters can come now," Koby said.

"Or else the monsters have no intention of coming here, and we're waiting for nothing," Halley said.

"Please, stop that complaining," Koby said to Halley.

As the night wore on, there was no sign of the monsters. Alice fell asleep leaning on Halley, and many of the others were also nodding off. The cold crept through their clothing. Minnie and Oscar kept looking at their watches and whispering. How much longer?

"They're not coming," Mimi declared suddenly. A few children who were half asleep woke up with a start. "Halley is right. They're not coming."

"Let's wait a little longer," Koby said.

"They're not coming," Mimi insisted. "I know it."

"Let's wait," Dad said. "They might still come. There's a full moon."

"I'm not waiting another second," Mimi snapped, and jumped to her feet. "I'm cold and hungry, and those dusty lumps aren't coming! I'm going now!"

"Just wait a minute," Dad said, trying to soothe her, but Mimi set off striding back toward the camp.

"Mimi, stop!" Dad yelled. Mimi stopped and turned to look back. "I'm coming with you," he said, and stood up.

At that very moment, a cracking sound came from

the forest. Something big and heavy was moving about nearby. Suddenly they were all wide awake.

"There—on the edge of the clearing, under the trees," Koby whispered, getting up. "Is something there?"

The rest of children clambered to their feet. Mimi took a few steps back toward the group. The last few yards she ran straight into Dad's arms.

Something big and gray was discernible in the shadows. Even if you had seen monsters in daylight, even if you had slept on the same living room floor and in the same camp as a monster, it was another thing altogether to see a whole pack of monsters in the eerie light of the full moon at the forest's edge. Even Dad looked nervous.

The monsters stepped out of the shadows into the clearing. They paid no attention to the watching children. In the small clearing in front of the rock, they began to circle each other. With a strange grace, they spun around one another, touched one another's hands, then continued moving without bumping into anybody. The earth was thumping with their heavy steps. Were they dancing?

The dance stopped almost as suddenly as it had begun. A dark figure moved to the front. It was Grah. Immediately another came to its side and stopped. Then a third, a fourth, a fifth . . .

"Look," Koby whispered. "That's the chain. They're forming a chain."

"I told you," Mimi said quietly from Dad's arms. "I told you what the bathrobe said."

The dark line of monsters stood motionless, as if waiting for something. Grah opened its huge hand, in which lay a crumpled ball.

"What is that?" Oscar whispered.

"Some paper?" Halley suggested, frowning. It was hard to see properly in moonlight.

"It's the page that was ripped out of Runar's book." Koby recognized it, amazed. "Look."

"It is?" Halley was doubtful.

Grah carefully smoothed the crumpled ball open.

"Grah took it, then?" Minnie whispered.

"Looks like it," said Koby.

All of a sudden he felt that he understood. He nodded to himself and said: "They needed Runar's monster to get home. Perhaps the picture is enough. Grah must have stayed behind in the camp because of that picture."

"What do you mean?" said Oscar.

"It had seen the picture and knew where it was. When the other monsters took off into the forest, Grah stayed to guard the book," Koby said. "Their return home depends on this picture."

Grah held up the drawing so that they could all see it. The monsters grunted approvingly. And—even though Koby's heart bled with the thought that a page had been

torn from a library book borrowed in his name — he was happy that the monster had been found. Even as a picture.

Grah raised the torn-out page high in the air and roared. The monsters understood. A few roared a reply; others stamped their feet on the ground and waved their thick arms.

"Oh, Grah," sobbed Mimi, as she understood that everything was over now. The monsters were going home. Tears ran down her cheeks.

Grah turned its yellow eyes to Mimi. It murred quietly. Mimi tore herself out of Dad's arms and ran across the clearing, once more to the arms of her dusty, sneeze-making, earth-cellar-scented friend. She breathed her lungs so full of monster dust that she almost choked. Or maybe it was her crying that was choking her. Grah squeezed Mimi in its arms and hummed like a big bees' nest, a deep, low hum.

"Mimi," Dad said quietly. "Come. Let them go. We don't know how much time they have or how long this will take. They must get to their home."

Mimi let go. Grah looked into Mimi's eyes and then put the girl down. Dad spread his arms, and Mimi ran like the wind right back into them and pressed her face against the shoulder of his jacket. Her little back shook with her sobs.

In the forest clearing, Grah turned back to the line of monsters. It raised the picture of Runar's monster up in the air and grunted: "Grah-ih-Gru!" The others echoed: "Grah-ih-Gru!"

Then Grah struck its chest with its hand and yelled: "Grah!" The others repeated its word. Next to Grah stood Oscar and Alice's monster, which struck its chest and shouted: "Grrr-hh-oo!" The others repeated.

"It had a name too," Oscar whispered. "We didn't know."

The monsters' roll call went on, rhythmic and ghostly. When the last call had sounded, the silence of the forest stunned their ears. Grah turned toward the rock and felt along the wall with its great hand. It found what it was searching for and knocked it with its fist. Something came off the wall. The monsters were growling their approval. Grah picked up the object as if to show the others.

"It looks like a plug off a boat," whispered Halley.

Mimi raised her head from the folds of Dad's jacket and turned to look.

Grah stepped to the edge of the rock, behind the fallen tree roots. The line of monsters followed. Grah reached up against the rock again, its fingers searching again for something on the rock surface. When it found the place, Grah murred. The monster choir replied.

"This could be scary, if one didn't know . . ." Dad said quietly. "If one didn't know that . . ."

He went quiet.

"That they're not dangerous," Koby filled in. "That they're just . . . like that, like themselves."

Dad nodded. That was it. Mimi got down from Dad's arms and turned to watch what Grah was doing. Grah reached up against the rock wall and knocked the plug in. There was a heavy grinding noise. The monsters stamped their feet and growled.

"The door to home is opening," Koby whispered.

"It is a sliding door after all," Alice said in a low voice.

Grah grunted and took the picture of Runar's monster. It held it out at arm's length, as if the picture were standing in its own place in the line. The monster chain was ready to leave.

All of a sudden, there was a scratching noise high up on top of the rock. A little shower of stones clattered down. The monsters' eyes turned toward the noise faster than a thought.

"Look!" exclaimed Minnie, and everybody looked. The sight was astonishing. In the eerie moonlight against the night sky, standing high up on the rock and looking down, was an old light gray monster. It was huge and strong, and one of its ears was torn. The wild, glowing eyes stared unblinking at the line of monsters in the clearing.

"Perhaps we should be going," Dad muttered. The monster nimbly leapt down from the rock. The leap would have seemed light, if the thud had not revealed the monster's weight. It stood now only a couple of yards from where Halley and Koby had been sitting.

The children stumbled backward. Dad yanked everybody, whomever he could reach, back from the clearing. But Runar's monster (for there was no doubt that it was Runar's monster) was not the least bit interested in humans. It stared at the other monsters, who stared back at it. The stare was expressionless and motionless, like monster staring always was. The moment stretched and lengthened. At last, Runar's monster took a cautious step toward the others.

"Grah-ih-Gru," grunted Grah in a low voice.

The rest of the pack repeated as a humming, low choir: "Grah-ih-Gru."

"Its name," Koby whispered. "They're greeting it by its name."

Grah-ih-Gru lowered its head and walked toward its place at the head of the chain. As it passed each monster, it touched them on the shoulder or outstretched hand with its hand, covered by gray, matted fur. Finally it took its rightful place at the head of the line.

Grah let Runar's drawing drop to the ground. Koby watched the paper drift down, relieved, but at the same time horrified. The page would be trampled by the monster pack.

Runar's monster let out a low grunt, and the others replied in chorus. Then the old monster turned, walked slowly behind the tree roots, and vanished. The chain of monsters was silent as they followed Runar's monster. Just before it vanished behind the roots, Grah raised its yellow eyes and looked at Mimi, as if to say goodbye. Mimi waved and let out a sob.

"The door is there," Koby whispered to Halley. "And that plug is the key. How does the door close?"

One after the other, the monsters disappeared from view. Last in line was Alba and Jenna's small gray monster. It stopped by the plug, grabbed it, and flung it into the forest.

The heavy sound of the closing door followed immediately. A clang, then another clang. The door to the